CONTENTS

Published in February, 1980,
by Seagull Publishing Co.,
3/F., Hip Sang Bldg., 107-111, Hennessy Road,
Hong Kong

Printed by Dragon View Off-Set Printing Co. Ltd.,
Block B, 7/F., Sum Lung Industrial Bldg.,
No. 11 Sun Yip Street, Chaiwan, Hong Kong

Heroes of the Marshes

In the neighbourhood of the monastery's vegetable fields were twenty or thirty worthless vagabonds and gamblers. They made their living by selling the vegetables they stole from the monastery's fields. One day when a few of them went to raid the fields, they observed a notice posted on the gate of the overseer's compound. It read:

The monastery has appointed the monk Lu Chih-shen overseer of these vegetable fields. Starting tomorrow, he shall be in charge. Those having no business here are strictly forbidden to enter.

The vagabonds then called a conference of the entire gang. "The monastery has sent a monk called Lu Chih-shen to take charge of the vegetable fields," they said. "He's new to the job. This is a good chance to pick a quarrel and beat him up. Teach the lout to respect us!"

"I have an idea," one of them said. "He doesn't know us; how can we pick a quarrel? Let's lure him to the edge of the ordure pit instead, kneel down as if to congratulate him, then grab his legs and toss him head over heels into the pit. It will be a nice little joke."

"Good! Good!" approved the vagabonds. After making their plans, they set out to seek the monk.

As to Lu Chih-shen, on arriving at the overseer's compound, he put his pack and luggage in the house, leaned his staff in a corner and hung up his dagger. The lay brothers who worked in the fields all came to greet him and he was handed the keys. The two monks who had escorted him there and the monk he was succeeding as overseer bade him farewell and returned to the monastery.

Chih-shen then made a tour of the vegetable fields. He saw coming towards him twenty or thirty vagabonds bearing a platter of pastries and ceremonial wine.

"We neighbours have heard that you've been put in charge, master monk," they said, grinning broadly, "and we've come to congratulate you."

Not knowing it was a plot, Chih-shen walked forward until he reached the edge of the ordure pit. The vagabonds advanced together, one of them intending to seize his left leg, another his right, and toss him in.

The result was: A foot kicked out and a fierce mountain tiger was startled; a fist struck out and a dragon of the sea met a sorry plight. A peaceful garden was instantly changed into a minor battlefield.

What came of the vagabonds' scheme to upset Chih-shen? If you want to know, listen to our next episode.

The Worldly Monk Uproots a Willow Tree
Lin Chung Enters White Tiger Council Hall by Mistake

As we were saying, among the twenty to thirty vagabonds who lived outside Sour Date Gate, two were leaders. One was "Rat Crossing the Street" Chang. The other was

"Snake in the Grass" Li. These two were in the lead as the gang advanced, Chih-shen naturally walked forward to meet them.

The gang halted at the edge of the ordure pit and chorused: "We've come to congratulate you on your new post."

"Since you're neighbours," said Chih-shen, "come into the compound and sit a while."

Chang and Li dropped to their knees respectfully. They hoped that the monk would approach to raise them courteously to their feet. Then they could go into action.

Noticing this, Chih-shen grew suspicious. "This gang is a queer-looking lot, and they're not willing to come forward. Can they be planning to dump me?" he wondered. "The louts think they can pluck the tiger's whiskers! Well, I'll go to them, and show them how I use my hands and feet!"

Chih-shen strode up to the gang. Still kneeling, Chang and Li cried, "We younger brothers have come especially to pay our respects," and each reached to grab one of the monk's legs. But before they could even lay a finger on him, Chih-shen lashed out with his right foot and kicked Li into the ordure pit; Chang rose to flee, but a quick thrust of the monk's left leg and the two rascals were floundering in the foul mess together.

Startled, the rest of the gang gaped, then turned to run.

"Whoever moves goes into the pit!" bellowed Chih-shen.

The vagabonds froze, not daring to take a step.

Chang and Li now raised their heads out of the ordure. The pit seemed bottomless, and they were covered with excrement. Maggots clung to their hair. Standing in the filth, they wailed. "Master, forgive us!"

"Help those two dogs out, you scoundrels," Chih-shen shouted to the gang, "and I'll forgive you all!"

The vagabonds quickly hauled their leaders from the pit and supported them over to a gourd arbour. The two stank to high heaven.

Chih-shen roared with laughter. "Fools! Go and wash off in the pond. Then I want to talk to all of you."

After the two gang leaders had cleansed themselves,

some of their men removed their own clothing to give them a change of garments.

"Come into the compound," Chih-shen ordered. "We're going to have a talk."

Sitting down in their midst, he pointed his finger at them and scoffed, "You ragamuffins! How could the likes of you ever hope to make sport of me?"

Chang, Li and the whole gang dropped to their knees. "Our families have lived here for generations," they said, "supporting themselves by gambling and begging and robbing these vegetable fields. The monastery paid people several times to drive us away, but no one could handle us. Where are you from, master monk? Such a terrific fellow! We've never seen you at the monastery before. From now on, we'll be happy to serve you."

"I'm from Yenan Prefecture, west of the Pass. I used to be a sergeant, under His Excellency the garrison commander. But because I killed many men, I took refuge in a monastery and became a monk. Before coming here, I was on Wutai Mountain. My family name is Lu. On entering the Buddhist order I was given the name Chih-shen. Even if surrounded by an army of thousands, I could hack my way out. What do you twenty or thirty amount to!"

Loudly and respectfully voicing their agreement with these sentiments, the vagabonds thanked the monk for his mercifulness and withdrew. Chih-shen went into the house, put his things in order, then went to bed.

The next day, after talking the matter over, the vagabonds scraped some money together and bought ten bottles of wine. Leading a live pig, they called on Chih-shen and invited him to join them in a feast. A table was laid in the overseer's compound. Chih-shen sat at the head of the table, with the twenty to thirty vagabonds lining both sides. Everyone drank.

"Why are you spending so much money?" the monk asked.

"We're lucky," they replied. "Now that you are here, you can be our master."

Chih-shen was very pleased. Wine flowed freely and the party grew gay. There was singing and talking and applause and laughter. Just as the merriment was at its height, crows were heard cawing outside the gate. Some of the men piously clacked their teeth and they intoned together: "Red lips rise to the sky, white tongue enters the earth."

"What are you making such a blasted racket about?" demanded Chih-shen.

The vagabonds replied: "When crows caw, it's a bad omen."

"Rot!" said the monk.

One of the lay brothers who tilled the monastery's fields laughed and said, "In the willow tree beside the wall there's a new crow's nest. The birds caw from dawn to dusk."

"Let's get a ladder and destroy the nest," said some.

"I'll do it," volunteered several of the others.

Feeling his wine, Chih-shen went out with the crowd to take a look. Sure enough, there was a crow's nest in the willow tree.

"Get a ladder and tear the nest down," said the men. "Then our ears can have a little peace and quiet."

"I'll climb up and do the job," boasted Li, "and I don't need any ladder."

Chih-shen looked the situation over, walked up to the tree and removed his tunic. Bending and grasping the lower part of the trunk with his right hand, while his left hand seized it higher up, he gave a tremendous wrench — and pulled the tree from the ground, roots and all!

The vagabonds dropped to their knees, crying: "The master is no ordinary mortal! He's truly one of the *Lohans*! If he didn't have ten million catties of strength, how could he have uprooted that tree?"

"It was nothing at all," said Chih-shen. "One of these days I'll show you how to handle weapons."

That night the vagabonds departed. But they came again the next day, and every day thereafter, bringing meat and wine to feast Chih-shen, for they positively worshipped him. They begged the monk to demonstrate his skill with weapons.

After several days of this, Chih-shen thought to himself: "These fellows have been treating me day after day. I ought to give them a banquet in return." He sent a few lay brothers into the city to buy several platters of pastries and five or six buckets of wine, and he killed a pig and slaughtered a sheep. It was then the end of the third lunar month.

"The weather's getting warm," said Chih-shen. He had mats spread beneath the green ash tree and invited the vagabonds to sit around and feast outdoors.

Wine was served in large bowls and meat in big chunks. When everyone had eaten his fill, the pastries were brought out and more wine. Soon the feasters were thoroughly sated.

"The past few days you've demonstrated your hand-to-hand fighting, master," said the vagabonds, "but you still haven't shown us your skill with weapons. It would be fine if you could give us a performance."

"All right," said Chih-shen. He went into the house and brought out his solid iron Buddhist staff, five feet long from end to end and weighing sixty-two catties.

His audience was amazed. "Only a man with the strength of a water buffalo in his arms could handle such a weapon!" they cried.

Chih-shen took up the staff and flourished it effortlessly, making it whistle through the air. At the sight of this, the vagabonds cheered and applauded.

Just as the monk was warming up, a gentleman appeared at a gap in the compound wall. "Truly remarkable!" he commended. Chih-shen stopped his exercise and turned to see who had spoken.

The gentleman wore a black muslin cap with its two corners gathered together; a pair of interlinked circlets of white jade held the knot of hair at the back of his head. He was dressed in a green officer's robe of flowered silk, bound at the waist by a girdle made of double strips of beaver and fastened by a silver clasp shaped like a tortoise back. His feet were shod in square-toed black boots. In his hand he carried a folding Chengtu fan. About thirty-five years old, he had a head like a panther, round eyes, a chin sharp as a swallow's beak, whiskers like a tiger, and stood six feet tall.

"Indeed remarkable," he said. "What excellent skill!"

"If he approves, it certainly must be good," said the vagabonds.

Lu Chih-shen displays his skill Ming dynasty woodcut

"Who is that officer?" queried Chih-shen.

"An arms instructor of the Eight Hundred Thousand Imperial Guards. His name is Lin Chung."

"Invite him in. I'd like to meet him."

Hearing this, the arms instructor leaped in through the gap in the wall. The two men greeted each other and sat down beneath the ash tree.

"Where are you from, brother monk?" asked Lin. "What is your name?"

"I'm Lu Ta, from west of the Pass. Because I killed many men, I had to become a monk. In my youth, I spent some time in Kaifeng, the eastern capital. I know your honourable father, Sergeant Lin."

Lin Chung was very pleased, and adopted Chih-shen as his sworn brother on the spot.

"What brings you here today?" asked Chih-shen.

"My wife and I just arrived at the Yueh Temple next door to burn incense. Hearing the cheers of your audience, I looked over and was intrigued by your performance. I told my wife and her maidservant, Chin Erh, to burn the incense without me, that I would wait for them by the gap in the wall. I didn't think I would actually have the honour to meet you, brother."

"When I first came to Kaifeng I didn't know anybody," said Chih-shen. "Then I became acquainted with these brothers and we gather together every day. Today, you have thought well enough of me to make me your sworn brother. That makes me very happy." He ordered the lay brothers to bring more wine.

Just as they were finishing their third round, the maidservant Chin Erh, agitated and red in the face, rushed up to the gap in the wall and cried: "Hurry, master! Our lady is having trouble with a man in the temple!"

"Where?" Lin Chung demanded hastily.

"As we were coming down the stairs of the Five Peaks Pavilion, a low fellow suddenly blocked her way. He won't let her pass!"

Lin Chung quickly took his leave of Chih-shen. "I'll see you again, brother. Forgive me!" He leaped through the gap in the wall and raced with Chin Erh back to the temple.

When he reached the Five Peaks Pavilion he saw several idlers carrying cross-bows, blow pipes and limed sticks gathered below the stair railing. They were watching a young man who was standing on the stairway with his back to them, blocking the path of Lin Chung's wife.

"Let's go upstairs," the young man was urging her. "I want to talk to you."

Blushing, the lady said, "What right do you have to make sport of a respectable woman in times of peace and order!"

Lin pushed forward, seized the young man by the shoulder and spun him around. "I'll teach you to insult a good man's wife," he shouted, raising his fist. Then he recognized Young Master Kao, adopted son of the Marshal in command of the entire military district.

When Marshal Kao Chiu had first risen to his high office he had no son to help him run his numerous affairs. And so he adopted the son of his younger brother. Since the boy was not only his nephew but now also his foster son, Marshal Kao loved him to excess.

The young scoundrel made full use of his foster father's influence in Kaifeng; his favourite pastime was despoiling other people's wives. Fearful of his powerful connections, none of the husbands dared speak out against him. He became known as the "King of Lovers."

After spinning him around, when Lin Chung saw that he was Young Master Kao, the strength left his arms.

"This has nothing to do with you, Lin Chung," said Kao. "Who asked you to interfere!" He didn't realize that the lady was Lin Chung's wife. Had he known, the thing would never have happened. Seeing Lin Chung's hesitancy, he spoke up boldly.

The commotion drew a crowd of idlers. "Don't be angry, arms instructor," one said. "The young master didn't recognize her. It was all a mistake."

Lin Chung's rage hadn't fully abated, and he glared at the rake with burning eyes. Some of the crowd soothed Lin Chung while others persuaded Kao to leave the temple grounds, get on his horse and depart.

Leading his wife and Chin Erh, the maidservant, Lin Chung was also turning to go when Chih-shen, iron staff in hand, came charging into the temple compound with huge strides, leading his twenty to thirty vagabonds.

"Where are you going, brother?" asked Lin Chung.

"I've come to help you fight!" said Chih-shen.

"The man turned out to be the son of our Marshal Kao. He hadn't recognized my wife and behaved discourteously. I was going to give the lout a good drubbing, but then I thought it would make the Marshal lose too much face," Lin Chung explained. "You know the old saying, 'Don't fear officialdom — but beware of the official who's over you.' After all, I'm on his payroll. I decided to let the young rascal off this time."

"You may be afraid of the Marshal of the district, but he doesn't scare me a bit!" shouted Chih-shen. "If I ever run into that young whelp of his I'll give him three hundred licks of my iron staff!"

Lin Chung saw that Chih-shen was drunk and he said placatingly, "You're quite right, of course, brother. It was only because everybody urged me that I let him go."

"The next time you have any trouble, just call me and I'll take care of it!"

The vagabonds supported the tipsy Chih-shen under the arms. "Let's go back, master," they said. "You can deal with young Kao later."

Raising his iron staff, Chih-shen said politely to Lin Chung's lady, "Your pardon, sister-in-law. Please don't laugh at me." And to Lin Chung he said, "Until tomorrow, brother." Then he and the vagabonds departed.

Lin Chung, his wife and Chin Erh returned home. The arms instructor was angry and depressed.

As for Young Master Kao, when he had drifted into the temple leading his band of idle cronies and met Lin Chung's wife, he had become sorely enamoured. After Lin Chung drove him off, he returned unhappily to the Marshal's Residence.

A few days later, his ne'er-do-well friends called. But they found him so fretful and irritable that they all went away again.

One of these idlers was an attendant named Fu An, better known as "Dried Pecker Head." Suspecting what was troubling Young Master Kao, he later went alone to the Residence. The young rake was sitting abstracted in the study. Fu An drew near and said:

"You've been rather pale lately, Young Master. You seldom smile. Something must be bothering you."

"How do you know?"

"I'm just guessing."

"Can you guess what it is?"

"Lin Chung's wife. How's that for a guess?"

The Young Master laughed. "Not bad. The problem is I don't know how to get her."

"Nothing to it! You're afraid to provoke Lin Chung because he's a big powerful fellow. But you needn't worry. He's under the Marshal's military command here. He has to behave courteously and watch his step. If he offends the Marshal, the least that can happen to him is exile; the worst is death. Now I've got a little scheme that will put his wife right into your hands."

"I've met many beautiful women. Why should I love only her? My heart is bewitched; I'm not happy. If you have a scheme that will work, I'll reward you generously."

"One of your trusted stewards, Lu Chien, is Lin Chung's best friend. Tomorrow, spread a feast in a quiet nook upstairs in Lu Chien's house. Then have Lu go to Lin and invite him out for some drinking; let Lu take him to a secluded room on the upper floor of the tavern. I'll go to Lin's wife and say, 'Your husband was drinking in Lu Chien's house when he was stricken by a sudden illness. He's collapsed. You'd better hurry and look after him!' Then I'll bring her over. Women are as changeable as water. When she sees what a handsome romantic sort you are, Young Master, and you deluge her with sweet words, she won't be able to resist. What do you think of my plan?"

"Excellent!" Kao applauded. "Have Lu Chien summoned here tonight."

It so happened that Lu Chien lived only one street away from the Kao Residence. He agreed to the scheme immediately; he felt he had no alternative. As long as it would please the Young Master, he was willing to forget about his friendship with the arms instructor.

To get back to Lin Chung. For several days he had been brooding at home. One morning he heard someone shouting at his front door, "Is the arms instructor in?"

Lin Chung went to the door, and there was Lu Chien.

"What brings you here, Brother Lu?" Lin asked quickly.

"I'm concerned about you. Why haven't I seen you on the streets these past few days, brother?"

"My mind is troubled. I don't feel like going out."

"Come and have a few cups with me and forget about your trouble."

"First sit a while and have some tea."

After the two finished their tea, they rose.

"Sister-in-law," Lu Chien called to Lin Chun's wife who was in the next room, "I'm taking Brother Lin over to my place for a few cups of wine."

The lady hurried to the door curtain. Pushing it aside, she admonished, "Don't let him drink too much, brother, and send him home early."

As the two men were strolling down the street, Lu Chien said, "Let's not go to my house, brother. We can have our drinks in the tavern."

And so they went to the public house. After selecting a small room, they ordered two bottles of good wine and some pastries to go with it. They chatted idly for a time. Lin Chung sighed.

"What's wrong, brother?" asked Lu Chien.

"You don't know what's happened! I have talents but they're not recognized by my superiors. I serve under little men from whom I have to take a lot of dirty nonsense!"

"There are several arms instructors in the Imperial Guards, but none can compare with you. The Marshal regards you very highly; who would dare to molest you?"

Lin Chung told Lu Chien about his encounter with Young Master Kao a few days before.

"The Young Master didn't realize she was your wife," Lu Chien said soothingly. "Forget it. Let's drink."

After downing eight or nine cups, Lin Chung had to relieve himself. Rising, he said, "I have to wash my hands." He went down the stairs, left the tavern, then attended to his business in a small lane to the east. Coming back out of the lane, he met Chin Erh.

"I've been looking all over for you, master!" said the maidservant. "So you're here!"

"What's up?" asked Lin Chung hastily.

"You had only been gone a little while when a man came rushing over to our house and said to the mistress, 'I'm a neighbour of Steward Lu. While drinking with Lu Chien, the arms instructor suddenly gasped for breath and fell to the floor! You'd better go and look after him.' Our lady begged Dame Wang next door to take care of our house, then she and I hastened with the man to a place one street past the Marshal's Residence. When we got upstairs we saw a table laden with food and drink, but there was no sign of you, master. As we turned to leave, that young fellow who pestered the mistress at the temple the other day came out and said, 'Stay a while, lady. I am your husband.' I flew down the stairs. Our mistress was screaming for help. But I couldn't find you anywhere. Finally I met Doctor Chang, the medicine vendor, and he told me, 'I just saw the arms instructor and another man going into the tavern.' So I hurried over here. Master, go quickly!"

Shocked, Lin Chung without waiting for Chin Erh, ran at triple speed to Lu Chien's house and raced up the stairs. The door was locked. He could hear his lady exclaiming, "In times of peace and order how dare you hold a good man's wife prisoner!" Young Master Kao was entreating, "Have pity on me, mistress! Even a woman of iron and stone shouldn't be so cold-hearted!"

"Wife, open the door!" thundered Lin Chung.

Hearing her husband's voice, Mistress Lin rushed to comply. The terrified Young Master Kao pushed open a window, climbed out and fled along the top of a wall. He was gone before Lin Chung entered the room.

"Did that dog violate you?" demanded the arms instructor.

"No," replied his wife.

In a fury, Lin Chung smashed Lu Chien's furniture to bits, then led his wife down the stairs. As they came out of the house, frightened neighbours on both sides of the street hastily shut their doors tight. Chin Erh was waiting for them outside. The three of them went home together.

Then, arming himself with a long sharp knife, Lin Chung sped directly to the tavern, seeking Lu Chien. But his treacherous friend was gone. Lin Chung next went to Lu Chien's house. Although he waited outside the door all night, Lu Chien did not return. Finally the arms instructor went home.

"He didn't harm me. Don't do anything foolish," his wife urged.

"Who would have thought that Lu Chien is such a scoundrel!" fumed Lin Chung. "Calling me 'brother' while plotting against me all the time! And when I catch that Young Master I'll give him a dose of the same medicine I'm going to give Lu Chien!"

Pleading desperately, his wife tried to keep Lin Chung at home.

Meanwhile, Lu Chien hid in the Marshal's Residence, afraid to return to his own house. For three successive days, the arms instructor waited for him outside the Residence gate, but the traitor didn't dare show himself. Lin Chung's appearance was so menacing, no one had the courage to question him.

On the fourth day since they parted, Chih-shen came to Lin Chung's home. "Where have you been keeping yourself these past few days, arms instructor?" the monk asked.

"I've been too busy to call on you, brother," replied Lin Chung apologetically. "Since you've honoured me with a visit to my humble home, I ought to offer you a few cups of wine. But we don't have anything decent to drink in the house. Why not go out for a stroll together and have a cup or two in the market place?"

"Excellent," said Chih-shen.

They went out and drank together all day and arranged to meet again on the morrow. Thereafter, Lin drank with Chih-shen every day. In time, he gradually set the other matter aside.

As to Young Master Kao, after he received that fright in Lu Chien's house and had to flee over the wall, he became ill and took to his bed. He didn't dare say anything to the Marshal about what had happened. Lu Chien and Fu An called on the Young Master at the Residence. They found him pale and in low spirits.

"Why are you so unhappy, Young Master?" asked Lu Chien.

"I won't try to fool you two," Kao replied. "After failing in both attempts to get Lin's wife, and then having that awful scare in addition, I feel worse than ever. If I pass out of this world in three months or half a year, you needn't be surprised!"

"Be of good cheer," the sycophants urged. "Unless she suddenly dies, we guarantee to get you that woman, come what may."

At that moment the old chamberlain entered to see how the Young Master was faring. Lu Chien and Fu An withdrew and held a private consultation. "There's only one way, . . ." they agreed. After the chamberlain had concluded his call and emerged, they invited him to a quiet corner and said:

"There's only one way the Young Master can get well. We must let the Marshal know and have him order the death of Lin Chung. Then the Young Master will be able to get Lin's wife and he'll recover. Otherwise, he's sure to die."

"That's easy," replied the old chamberlain. "I'll inform the Marshal this evening."

"We already have a plan," said the two. "We only await word from you."

That night, the old chamberlain saw the Marshal. "I've discovered what's wrong with the Young Master," he said. "It's Lin Chung's wife."

"When did he ever see the woman?" asked the Marshal.

"On the twenty-eighth of last month, at Yueh Temple. Today is a little over a month," said the old chamberlain, and he told the Marshal what Lu Chien had in mind.

"H'mm, Lin Chung's wife, eh? The question is how to put Lin Chung out of the way, . . ." mused the Marshal. "Let me think. I can't let my son lose his life just for the sake of Lin Chung."

"Lu Chien and Fu An have a plan."

"So? Bring them in here and we'll talk it over."

The old chamberlain summoned Lu Chien and Fu An into the Marshal's hall. They hailed him respectfully.

"Do you two have a plan that can cure my son's illness? If so, I will raise you both in rank."

Lu Chien stepped forward. "Gracious lord, it can be done only thus and thus and thus. . . ."

"Very well," said the Marshal. "You may take action tomorrow."

Of this we need say no more.

To get back to Lin Chung. Drinking every day with Chih-shen, he finally forgot about the matter.

One day, as the two friends were nearing a lane, they saw a big fellow standing on the corner, a cap with gathered ends on his head and dressed in an old military robe. He was holding a fine sword in his hand, with a tuft of grass tied to it indicating that it was for sale.

"No one recognizes its value," he was muttering. "What a pity for my precious sword!"

Lin Chung paid no attention and continued walking and chatting with Chih-shen. The man trailed behind them, saying:

"A splendid sword. It's a shame that no one appreciates it!"

Lin Chung and Chih-shen were still engrossed in their conversation. Following them, the man cried:

"A big city like the eastern capital and not a single person knows the worth of military weapons!"

At this, Lin Chung looked around. The fellow whipped the sword out of its sheath. It gleamed dazzlingly in the sun. Lin Chung was fated for trouble. He said abruptly:

"Let me see it!"

The fellow handed him the sword. Lin Chung took the weapon and he and Chih-shen examined it. Astonished, the arms instructor exclaimed:

"An excellent blade! How much do you want for it?"

"The price is three thousand strings of cash, but I'll take two."

"It's well worth two thousand, but you won't find anyone who'll give that much. If you're willing to accept one thousand, I'll buy it from you."

"I need money quickly. If you really want the sword I'll knock off five hundred and let you have it for fifteen hundred."

"A thousand is the best I can do."

The fellow sighed. "It's selling gold at the price of iron. All right, all right, but not one copper less."

"Come home with me and I'll give you the money," said Lin Chung. Turning to Chih-shen, he proposed, "Wait for me in the tea-house, brother. I'll join you soon."

"No," said the monk, "I must go back. I'll see you tomorrow."

After taking leave of Chih-shen, Lin Chung brought the sword-seller to his home, counted out the purchase price in silver and gave it to him.

"Where did you get this blade?" the arms instructor asked.

"It was handed down to me from my ancestors. Because my family became impoverished I had no choice. I had to sell it."

"What's the name of your family?"

"If I were to tell you, I'd die of shame!"

Lin Chung asked no more. The fellow took the money and departed.

Turning the sword this way and that, Lin Chung exclaimed admiringly, "Truly a beautiful weapon! Marshal Kao is supposed to have a fine sword but he won't show it to anyone. Though I've asked to see it several times, he's never been willing to bring it out. Today I've bought a fine sword too. One of these days I'll compare blades with him."

The arms instructor didn't let the sword out of his hand all evening. Late that night he finally hung it on the wall, but he was up before daybreak and took the blade down again to admire it.

Some time before noon two messengers came to his gate and cried, "Arms Instructor Lin, an order from the Marshal! He's heard that you've bought a fine sword and wants you to bring it to compare it with his. The Marshal is waiting for you in the Residence."

"Who is the big-mouthed gossip that reported the news so fast!" wondered Lin Chung.

The messengers waited while Lin Chung got dressed. Taking his sword, the arms instructor accompanied them. On the way he said to the messengers:

"I haven't seen you at the Residence before."

"We've only recently been transferred," they replied.

Soon they arrived at the Residence. In the reception room, Lin Chung halted.

"The Marshal is waiting in the rear hall," said the messengers.

Lin Chung went with them around a screen wall into the rear hall. But there was still no sign of the Marshal, and Lin Chung halted once more.

"The Marshal is awaiting the arms instructor in the rearmost court. He directed us to bring you there," said the messengers.

Lin followed them through two or three more doorways until they came to a courtyard lined on all sides by green railings. The messengers led him to the entrance of a large hall and said:

"Please wait out here, arms instructor, while we report to the Marshal. We won't be long."

Lin Chung stood before the eaves while the two messengers went inside. A time long enough to drink a cup of tea passed, but they did not return. Growing suspicious, the arms instructor pushed aside a hanging awning, poked his head in and looked. There, above the door, was a placard with four words written in green: "White Tiger Council Hall."

"This is where the highest military affairs are discussed," thought Lin Chung, startled. "How dare I go in there!"

As he was hastily turning, he heard the tread of boots behind him, the steps ringing sharply. Another man had entered the courtyard. The arms instructor recognized him. It was none other than Marshal Kao, commander of the district. Profferring his sword with both hands, Lin Chung greeted him respectfully.

"Lin Chung!" the Marshal barked. "I didn't summon you: how dare you force your way into the White Tiger Council Hall! Don't you know the law? And carrying a weapon! You must have come to kill me! People told me that you were seen waiting outside the Residence two or three days ago with a knife in your hand. Your intentions are surely evil!"

Bowing, Lin Chung replied, "Benevolent lord, two of your messengers brought me here saying you wanted to compare your sword with mine."

"Where are the messengers?" cried the Marshal.

"They just went into the hall, sir."

"Lies! Lies! No messenger would dare enter my official halls! Ho, guards! Seize this lout!"

Before the order had left the Marshal's mouth, from the buildings flanking the sides of the courtyard over thirty stalwarts came rushing out and knocked Lin Chung to the ground.

"As an arms instructor of the Imperial Guards, you must know the law," the Marshal raged. "Why else would you enter the Council Hall with a sharp sword in your hand if not to murder me?"

He ordered his men to take Lin Chung away. Could Lin Chung survive?

And because of this there was a great tumult on the Central Plains and a wild disturbance on the waters. Peasants had to wear army designations on their backs; military pennants fluttered on fishing boats.

If you want to know whether Lin Chung lived or died, then listen to our next episode.

Arms Instructor Lin Is Tattooed and Exiled to Tsangchou
Lu Chih-shen Makes a Shambles of Wild Boar Forest

As we were saying, Marshal Kao shouted for his guards to take Lin Chung out and execute him. Lin Chung loudly exclaimed that he was innocent.

"Why did you enter the Council Hall with a sword in your hand?" demanded the Marshal. "Of course you wanted to kill me!"

"Would I dare go in if the Marshal hadn't summoned me?" countered Lin Chung. "I saw those two messengers enter the hall. They tricked me into coming here."

"Nonsense! What messengers are you talking about? This scoundrel refuses to admit his guilt!" said the Marshal. And he directed his guards, "Take him to the Kaifeng Prefecture; ask Prefect Teng to examine him and investigate the case. Get the truth out of him, then have him executed! Label the sword as an official exhibit and take it along!"

Bearing the Marshal's order, the guards escorted Lin Chung to the Kaifeng Prefecture. It happened that the prefect was still holding court, and Marshal Kao's emissary brought Lin Chung into the prefect's hall and knelt at the foot of the dais. The prefect's secretary relayed the emissary's message from Marshal Kao and placed the labelled sword down in front of Lin Chung.

"Lin Chung," said the prefect, "you're an arms instructor in the Imperial Guards. You must know the law. How could you enter the Council Hall holding a sword? That's an offence punishable by death!"

"Benevolent lord, you reflect the truth like a mirror. Lin Chung has been grievously wronged! Although I'm only a crude and stupid military man, I'm not exactly ignorant of the law. How would I presume to enter the Council Hall? The reason I went there was this: On the twenty-eighth of last month I took my wife to Yueh Temple to burn incense. There I caught Marshal Kao's son trying to seduce her. I berated him and drove him away. Next, he had Steward Lu trick me into going out to drink and got Fu An to lure my wife to Steward Lu's home, where he tried to ravish her. This too I discovered and wrecked Lu Chien's furniture. Though Young Master Kao failed to despoil her, I have witnesses to both attempts.

"Yesterday, I bought this sword. Today, Marshal Kao sent two messengers to summon me; they said he wanted me to bring my sword to compare it with his. And so I went with them to the Council Hall. After they went inside, Marshal Kao suddenly entered the courtyard. It's all a plot to destroy me. Please help me, Your Honour!"

After hearing Lin Chung's story, the prefect ordered that a receipt-of-prisoner be issued, a wooden cangue locked around the arms instructor's neck, and that he be held in custody. Lin Chung's family sent food to him in gaol and gave tips to the keepers. His father-in-law, Arms Instructor Chang, also called at the prison. He spent quite a bit, bribing high and low.

It happened that in the prefecture there was a record clerk named Sun Ting. Because he was extremely just and kindly and always willing to help people, he was known as Sun the Buddha. Learning the facts of the case, he diplomatically informed the prefect what he had discovered.

"Lin Chung has been wronged," he said. "You must help him."

"But Marshal Kao has confirmed that he committed a crime. He insists that I convict Lin Chung for entering the Council Hall, sword in hand, with the intention of murdering him. What can I do?"

"The sovereign office of the Kaifeng Prefecture belongs not to the royal court but to the family of Marshal Kao!"

"Not at all!"

"Everyone knows Marshal Kao uses his position tyrannically. There's nothing he won't do. Whoever offends him, even in the slightest, he sends to the Kaifeng Prefecture. If he wants a man killed, we kill him; if he wants him hacked, we hack him. We've become a mere subdivision of his family!"

"How can I make things easy for Lin Chung? What sort of sentence should I pass?"

"From Lin Chung's story, it's plain that he's innocent, although we haven't been able to find those two messengers. Why not have him confess to entering the Council Hall improperly wearing a sword at his waist, sentence him to twenty strokes of the bamboo, tattoo him and exile him to some distant military district?"

After considering this, Prefect Teng went to see Marshal Kao and urged him to agree to such a confession from Lin Chung. Knowing that reason was against him, and since the prefect seemed reluctant to co-operate, the Marshal was forced to consent.

The very same day, the prefect called court into session. He had Lin Chung summoned, the cangue removed and twenty blows of the bamboo administered. After directing the tattooer to place the mark of a criminal on Lin Chung's cheek, the prefect calculated the distance and decided upon Tsangchou as Lin's place of exile. In full court, a hinged wooden cangue of seven and a half catties was placed around the arms instructor's neck, and nailed fast, and prefectural seals were affixed. The prefect then issued a deportation order and designated two constables to escort the prisoner to his destination. Their names were Tung Chao and Hsueh Pa.

On receiving the order, together with Lin Chung, the constables left the prefectural compound. Outside the gate, many of Lin Chung's neighbours and his father-in-law, Arms Instructor Chang, were waiting. All repaired to a tavern at Chouchiao Bridge and took seats.

"Thanks to the assistance of Record Clerk Sun, my beating was not heavy and I'm still able to walk," said Lin Chung.

Arms Instructor Chang told the waiter to serve the two constables with wine and pastries. After they had drunk several cups, the old man presented them each with some silver.

Clasping hands respectfully, Lin Chung addressed his father-in-law.

"Bad times have befallen me, exalted father-in-law. I clashed with Young Master Kao and the court has condemned me wrongfully. Now I have something to say: In the three years since you generously gave me your daughter in marriage she has never done anything to displease me. Although she's borne no children, not once have we quarrelled or even grown red in the face. Today I've suffered this misfortune. I'm being exiled to Tsangchou and there's no telling whether I'll live or die. My lady will be left at home. I'm worried about her, I'm afraid Young Master Kao will try to force his suit.

"She's still young; I shouldn't tie her down. This is my own idea, it's entirely voluntary. In the presence of our honourable neighbours I want to write out an annulment of our marriage, consenting to her making a new match and promising not to contest it. Only in this way will I feel at ease, assured that Young Master Kao won't be able to harm her."

"What words are these, good son-in-law!" cried the old arms instructor. "You've been unlucky and this misfortune has happened. It's not of your own doing. Today you're going to Tsangchou for temporary refuge, but sooner or later Heaven will pity you and let you return, and husband and wife will be together again. I've got a bit of money; I'll have my daughter and Chin Erh move in with me. Come what may, I can support them for four or five years. I won't allow my daughter out on the streets. Young Master Kao won't be able to see her even if he wants to. Don't worry. I'll take care of everything. You go on to Tsangchou. From time to time I'll send you letters and clothing. Don't get any foolish ideas. Just go in peace."

"Thank you, father-in-law, for your good intentions. But I wouldn't feel right, tying her down. Have pity, father-in-law, let me have my way. Then, even if I die, I can close my eyes peacefully!"

But Arms Instructor Chang wouldn't hear of it. The neighbours also were opposed.

"Unless I am allowed to do this, even if I succeed in coming back I swear I'll never see her again!" said Lin Chung.

"Write out the annulment, if that's how you feel," said the old man. "In any event, I won't let my daughter marry another."

Lin Chung then sent for a scribe and purchased a sheet of paper. The scribe wrote as Lin Chung dictated:

> *Because he was convicted of a serious crime, Lin Chung, arms instructor of the Imperial Guards, eastern capital, has been sentenced to exile in Tsangchou. What will happen to him is difficult to foretell. His wife (maiden name Chang) is still young, and he therefore wishes to annul their marriage. He grants her permission to contract a new marriage and guarantees that he will never contest it. The annulment is truly voluntary and not issued under compulsion. In the event of any doubt, this document shall serve as proof.*
>
> *Year . . . Month . . . Day . . .*

When the document was completed, Lin Chung took the writing brush and signed his name below the date, then added his thumb print. Just as he was about to hand the annulment to his father-in-law, his wife, weeping and crying aloud, came hurrying to the tavern, followed by the maidservant, Chin Erh, who was carrying a bundle of clothing. Lin Chung rose and went forward to meet her.

"Wife," he said, "I have something to tell you. I've already spoken to father-in-law. Because I've fallen on bad times, I've had this misfortune. Today, I start for Tsangchou. It's hard to say whether I'll live or die. I don't want to hold you back in the flower of your youth, so I've had this document written. Please don't wait for me. If you meet a good man, marry again. Don't delay your happiness on my account."

"Husband!" she wept. "I've never wronged you in the slightest. How can you discard me?"

"I mean well, wife," said Lin Chung. "Otherwise, we'll only impede each other. You'll be harmed."

"Don't worry, my daughter," said Arms Instructor Chang. "Even though son-in-law recommends it, I'll never allow you to remarry. He can depart easy in his mind. If he doesn't return, I'll provide for you for the rest of your life, as long as you're willing to remain faithful to him."

The young woman uttered heart-rending sobs. Tears streaming down her cheeks, when she saw the annulment document she collapsed swooning to the floor. Lin Chung and his father-in-law hurried to raise her. It was some time before she revived. She wept uncontrollably as Lin Chung presented the document to her father. Women neighbours did their best to comfort her. Supporting the bereft woman under the arms, they escorted her home.

"Go, and try to come back soon," Arms Instructor Chang told Lin Chung. "Tomorrow, I shall move your wife over to my house. I'll take care of her until your return. You can depart without any worries. Be sure to write to us from time to time, if you find people who can deliver your letters."

Lin Chung rose and thanked his father-in-law and his neighbours, placed his bundle on his back, and went off with the constables. Arms Instructor Chang and the neighbours departed for home; of them we shall say no more.

We'll speak of the two constables and Lin Chung. After locking their prisoner in a guard house, Tung Chao and Hsueh Pa returned to their homes to pack some things for their journey. As Tung Chao was tying a bundle together, a waiter from the tavern at the head of the lane came and said:

"Sir, a gentleman wishes to speak with you in our tavern."

"Who is he?"

"I don't know him. He only told me to invite you over."

Tung Chao went with the waiter to a room in the tavern. He found a man wearing a hat decorated with Buddhist swastikas and dressed in a black silk tunic; on his feet were black boots and plain stockings. When Tung Chao entered, the man quickly rose and clasped hands in greeting.

"Please be seated, sir," he said.

"I have not had the privilege of meeting Your Honour before," said Tung Chao. "How can I serve you?"

"Please sit down. You'll know shortly."

Tung Chao took a chair on the opposite side of the table. The waiter brought wine cups and food and pastries and laid them out.

"Where does Constable Hsueh live?" the man asked.

"In that lane ahead," replied Tung Chao.

The man called the waiter and asked him for Hsueh's exact address. "Invite him here to meet me," he instructed.

In less time than it takes to drink a cup of tea, the waiter returned with Hsueh Pa.

"This gentleman has invited us here for a talk," Tung Chao explained.

"May I ask your name, sir?" queried Hsueh Pa.

"You'll know very soon," replied the man. "First let us drink."

The three took their seats and the waiter served the wine. After they had consumed several cups, the man drew from his sleeve ten ounces of gold and placed them on the table.

"Five ounces for each of you two constables," he said. "There is a small matter I want to trouble you about."

"But we don't know Your Honour. Why should you give us gold?" they asked.

"Aren't you going to Tsangchou?"

"We're taking Lin Chung there under orders of the Kaifeng prefect," said Tung Chao.

"It's precisely for that reason that I must bother you two. I am Marshal Kao's trusted steward Lu Chien."

Tung Chao and Hsueh Pa immediately greeted him with profound respect. "How can insignificant men like us presume to sit at the same table with Your Honour!" they cried.

"As you know, Lin Chung has incurred the Marshal's displeasure. The Marshal has ordered me to present you with these ten ounces of gold. He hopes you will promise to finish off Lin Chung in some secluded place along the road — it needn't be too far — and bring back a certification of his death from the local authorities. If the Kaifeng Prefecture causes any difficulty, the Marshal will take care of it personally; you needn't worry about that."

"I'm afraid it's not possible," said Tung Chao. "The official order of the Kaifeng Prefecture directs that we deliver Lin Chung alive, not that we kill him. He's not an old man; how could we explain his death? We'd surely get into trouble. I'm afraid it can't be done."

"Tung, old man," said Hsueh Pa, "listen to me. If Marshal Kao ordered us to die, we would have to obey, to say nothing of a case like this, when he sends this gentleman to give us gold. Say no more. I'll share it with you and that's that. If we do this little favour, we'll be looked after in the future. On the road to Tsangchou is a big pine forest, a wild evil place. Come what may, we'll finish him off there!"

Hsueh Pa took the gold and said, "You can rely on us, Your Honour. At the latest on the fifth stage of the journey, at the earliest the second, the thing will be done."

Very pleased, Lu Chien exclaimed, "Constable Hsueh is truly straightforward and to the point! When the deed is accomplished, bring back the golden print on Lin Chung's face as proof. I will then reward you both with another ten ounces of gold. I shall be waiting for good news. Be sure not to delay."

In Sung times, prisoners who were to be exiled were always tattooed on the face. To make it sound better, the mark was called "the golden print."

The three finished their wine, Lu Chien paid the bill, then all left the tavern and went their separate ways.

Tung Chao and Hsueh Pa, after dividing the gold, returned to their homes and finished packing. Then they took their constables' staves, called for Lin Chung at the guard house, and set out from the city. They travelled more than thirty *li* before calling a halt. In Sung days, constables escorting a prisoner did not have to pay for lodging in public inns. Hsueh and Tung brought Lin Chung to an inn, and they stayed the night.

At dawn the next morning, the constables lit a fire and made breakfast, then the three continued their journey to

Tsangchou. It was the height of summer and the weather was scorching. Lin Chung had not suffered much when he was beaten. But now a few days had passed, and the fiery heat irritated his wounds. He walked painfully, with dragging steps.

"Stupid clod!" Hsueh Pa said. "It's over two thousand *li* from here to Tsangchou. Who knows when we'll get there, at the rate you're going!"

"I was buffeted a bit in the Marshal's compound, and then, the other day, I was beaten with bamboos. My wounds are paining me in this awful heat," Lin Chung explained. "Please, sirs, don't be impatient."

"Just take your time," said Tung Chao. "Never mind his grumbling."

Hsueh Pa kept complaining and cursing all along the road. "It's our misfortune to have run into a wretched demon like you!" he berated Lin Chung.

As the day was drawing to a close, the three again put up in a village inn. Entering the door, the constables rested their staves and removed their packs. Lin Chung also dropped his luggage bundle. Before the constables could say anything, he took out some pieces of silver and told the attendant to bring wine and meat and hot rice, and set them on the table. Lin then invited the constables to dine with him.

Tung Chao and Hsueh Pa ordered still more wine, plying Lin Chung with it until he fell over on his side, wooden cangue and all. Hsueh Pa then boiled a large pot of water. When it was bubbling hot he brought it out and poured it into a basin.

"Wash your feet, Arms Instructor Lin," he said. "You'll sleep better."

Lin Chung struggled to a sitting position, but he couldn't lean forward because of the cangue.

"I'll wash them for you," Hsueh Pa offered.

"How could I impose upon you!" Lin Chung hastily refused.

"Men travelling together shouldn't be ceremonious over such details!" said Hsueh Pa.

Not realizing it was a plot, Lin Chung stretched out his legs. Hsueh Pa seized them and plunged his feet into the boiling water.

"Aiya!" exclaimed Lin Chung, hurriedly pulling them out. His feet had turned red and swollen. "You needn't trouble!" he cried.

"Plenty of prisoners have looked after constables, but how often do you see a constable serving a prisoner!" said Hsueh Pa. "With the best of intentions I wash his feet, but he has the nerve to complain — the water's too cold; the water's too hot! If this isn't 'returning bad for good' I don't know what is!"

He grumbled and swore half the night.

Not daring to reply, Lin Chung could only fall over and lie on his side.

The two constables poured out the boiling water, filled the basin afresh, then went to wash their feet outside.

They slept until the fourth watch, rising while the rest of the inn was still in bed. Hsueh Pa heated some water to wash with, and cooked breakfast. Lin Chung, dizzy, was unable to eat and barely able to walk. Hsueh Pa threatened him with his staff. Tung Chao untied from his belt a pair of new straw sandals with loops and bindings of woven hemp. He told Lin Chung to put them on. Lin Chung's scalded feet were covered with blisters. He wanted his worn soft sandals, but they were nowhere to be found. He had to put the new ones on.

After the waiter had added up the bill, the constables led Lin Chung from the inn. It was by now the fifth watch.

Before Lin Chung had gone more than two or three *li*, the blisters on his feet, broken by the new straw sandals, bled freely. He could hardly drag himself along and he groaned ceaselessly.

"Walk! Faster!" shouted Hsueh Pa. "Keep moving or I'll help you with this staff!"

"Have pity on me, good officer!" Lin Chung pleaded. "Would I dare to slow down deliberately and delay our journey? It's because my feet are killing me. I can't walk!"

"You can lean on me," said Tung Chao. He supported Lin Chung and they struggled on another four or five *li*.

When it became obvious that Lin Chung really couldn't go much farther, they saw ahead of them a wild evil wood shrouded in mist. Known as Wild Boar Forest, it was the first dangerous place on the road from Kaifeng to Tsangchou. During the Sung dynasty, those who had grudges against prisoners being sent into exile often bribed their escorts to murder them. Who can say how many good men lost their lives in this wood?

Now, the two constables led Lin Chung straight into the forest.

"In five watches we can't even walk ten *li*," said Tung Chao. "We'll never reach Tsangchou at this rate!"

"I'm tired too," said Hsueh Pa. "Let's rest here in the woods."

After penetrating deeper into the forest, the three men removed their packs and placed them at the foot of a tree. Lin Chung groaned. With his back against a tree trunk he slid to the ground.

"Having to wait for you every time we take a step has worn us out," said the constables. "We'll sleep a while and then go on."

They rested their staves and lay down beside a tree. But no sooner had they closed their eyes than they leaped up with an exclamation.

"What's wrong, good officers?" asked Lin Chung.

"We were just about to sleep when we remembered that there are no doors and locks here. We're afraid you'll run off. We're worried, so we can't sleep in peace."

"I'm a respectable man. Since I've already been convicted, I'd never run away!"

"Who can believe that!" scoffed Hsueh Pa. "The only way we can really feel secure is to tie you up."

"If that's what you good officers want, how can I refuse?"

Hsueh Pa took a rope from his waist and bound Lin Chung hand and foot and tied him, together with the cangue, tightly to the tree. Then he and Tung Chao sprang up, whirled around, seized their staves and advanced on Lin Chung.

"Killing you isn't our idea," they said. "The other day Steward Lu informed us of the order of Marshal Kao: We're to finish you off here and return immediately with the golden print. Even if we travelled a few more days, it would still be your death march! Doing the job here, we can get back that much earlier. Don't blame us two brothers. We're only carrying out orders; we have no choice. You must know: A year from this day will be the first anniversary of your death! We've been given a time limit. We must return quickly with our report."

When Lin Chung heard this, his tears fell like rain. "Officers!" he cried. "There's never been any enmity between us. Spare me, and I'll never forget you in this world or the next!"

"Empty talk!" said Tung Chao. "You can't be saved!"

Hsueh Pa raised his constable's staff and swung it fiercely at Lin Chung's head.

What a pity for a hero to die thus with bound hands!

There are no inns on the long road to the nether regions. In whose home can a wandering spirit rest in the deep of night?

Did Lin Chung live or die? Listen to our next episode if you want to know.

Chai Chin Keeps Open House for All Bold Men
Lin Chung Defeats Arms Instructor Hung in a Bout with Staves

As we were saying, Hsueh Pa raised his staff with both hands to bring it down on Lin Chung's head. But quicker than words can tell, from behind the pine tree came a thunderous roar as a solid iron rod shot forward, intercepted the staff and sent it flying into the sky. Then out leaped a big fat monk.

"I heard everything you said!" he yelled. Dressed in a black cassock, he was wearing a big knife and carried a Buddhist staff which he brandished at the two constables.

Lin Chung, who had just opend his eyes, recognized Lu Chih-shen, and he hastily cried: "Brother! Stay your hand! I have something to say!"

Chih-shen lowered his iron staff. The constables gaped at him, too frightened to move.

"It's not their doing," said Lin Chung. "Marshal Kao, through Lu Chien, gave them orders to destroy me. How could they refuse? It would be wrong to kill them!"

Whipping out his knife, Chih-shen cut the arms instructor's bonds and helped him to his feet.

"Brother," he said, "I've been worried about you ever since that day we parted, when you bought the sword. After you were convicted, I had no way to rescue you. I heard that you were being exiled to Tsangchou, and I sought you outside the Kaifeng Prefecture, but in vain. Someone said that you had been locked in a guard house. Then I learned that a waiter had gone to the two constables, saying, 'A gentleman wishes to speak to you in the tavern,' and I became suspicious. I was afraid these oafs would try to harm you along the road, so I followed.

"When these knaves brought you to the inn, I put up there too. I heard them plotting in whispers. When they tricked you and scalded your feet in the boiling water, I wanted to kill them on the spot. But there were too many

Rescue in Wild Boar Forest Ming dynasty woodcut

guests at the inn and I was afraid I couldn't carry it off. I knew the rogues were up to something dirty; I was very worried.

"You set out before dawn at the fifth watch. I hurried ahead to the forest and waited to kill the two wretches here. They came here to harm you, so now I ought to destroy them!"

"Since you've saved me, brother, there's no need to kill them," urged Lin Chung.

"Scurvy knaves!" bellowed Chih-shen. "If it weren't for my brother here, I'd pound you both into mincement! Only because he asks it, I'll spare your lives!" He put his knife away and shouted, "Support my brother, and be quick about it! Come with me!" Taking his staff, he set off.

How dared they refuse? Crying, "Save us, Instructor Lin!" the constables again shouldered their packs and grasped their staves. Supporting Lin Chung and carrying his bundle, they followed the monk out of the forest.

After walking three or four *li*, they saw a little tavern at the entrance to a village. All four went in and sat down. They ordered five or six catties of meat, two jugs of wine and some griddle cakes. The waiter laid the table and served the wine.

"May we presume to inquire," the constables said to Chih-shen, "in what monastery you reside, master?"

Chih-shen chuckled. "Why do you ask, scoundrels? So that you can tell Marshal Kao how to harm me? Others may fear him; I don't! If I meet that wretch I'll give him three hundred licks of my iron staff!"

The constables dared say no more.

The four finished the meat and wine, got their luggage in order, paid the bill and left the village.

"Where are you planning to go today, brother?" asked Lin Chung.

" 'To kill a man you must draw blood, to rescue a man you must see him to safety.' I still don't feel at ease about you, brother. I'm going to escort you all the way to Tsangchou."

Hearing this, the two constables secretly groaned, "Woe! That ruins our scheme! What will we say when we get back?" But they could only continue the journey, docilely obeying the monk's orders.

From then on, they marched when he wanted to march, and rested when he wanted to rest. How dared they oppose him? In a good mood, he merely cursed them; in a bad, he beat them. Neither of the constables dared say a word for fear of arousing the monk's ire.

After marching two more stages, they hired a cart. Lin Chung rested on the cart, while the other three walked behind it. The constables had guilty consciences and were anxious to preserve their lives, so they tagged along cautiously.

On the road, Chih-shen frequently bought wine and meat for Lin Chung, and the constables were permitted to join him. When the party came to an inn, they would retire early and rise late. Of course, the constables lit the fires and did the cooking. Who dared to disobey the monk?

They conferred worriedly in private. "We've become the prisoners and the monk the escort. When we get back, Marshal Kao will surely punish us!"

"I've heard that a newly arrived monk has been put in charge of the monastery vegetable fields," said Hsueh Pa. "He's called Lu Chih-shen. This must be the man. Let's tell the truth when we get back. We'll say that we wanted to finish Lin Chung off in Wild Boar Forest, but that the monk rescued him and went with us all the way to Tsangchou; that was why we couldn't do the job. We'll return the ten ounces of gold to Lu Chien. Let him settle accounts with the monk himself. All you and I want is to be clear of the whole thing."

"My feelings exactly," said Tung Chao.

Of their discussion we shall say no more.

To make a long story short, they marched for seventeen or eighteen days, with Chih-shen never relaxing his watch over the two constables. Soon they were only about seventy *li* from Tsangchou. It was a well-travelled road the rest of the way; there were no desolate stretches. After inquiring to make sure of this, Chih-shen led the party into a grove to rest.

"Brother," he said to Lin Chung, "from here to Tsangchou is not far. There are plenty of people on the road and no deserted places. I've already checked on it. I'll part with you here. Some day we'll meet again."

"Go back, brother. Let my father-in-law know that I'm all right," said Lin Chung. "If I live, I'll repay you for your gracious protection in full."

Chih-shen took out a score or more pieces of silver and gave them to Lin Chung, then handed two or three pieces to the constables.

"Scurvy knaves! Originally I was going to cut your heads off along the road. Out of courtesy to my brother I've spared your paltry lives! The journey is nearly over. Don't get any evil ideas!"

"Would we dare?" replied the two. "It was all Marshal Kao's doing!" They accepted the silver and divided it between them.

As they turned to leave, Chih-shen glared and shouted, "Wretches! Are your heads harder than this pine tree?"

"We humble servants have heads only of the flesh and skin our parents gave us, wrapped around a few bones. . . ."

Chih-shen raised his iron staff and struck the tree a mighty blow, making a gash two inches deep. The pine folded over neatly and fell.

"Scurvy knaves!" roared the monk. "If you get any wrong ideas, I'll clout your heads like I did this pine!"

Dragging his iron staff with one hand and swinging his other arm, Chih-shen walked off, calling, "Take care of yourself, brother!"

"Let's go, good officers," said Lin Chung.

"Terrific!" exclaimed the constables. "With one blow he snaps a tree in half!"

"That's nothing," said Lin Chung. "Back in the monastery, he pulled a tree up by the roots."

The two constables wagged their heads. This confirmed their guess about the monk's identity.

Leaving the grove, the three continued walking until noon. Down the highway they observed a tavern. They entered, and Lin Chung invited the constables to sit at the head of the table. Tung and Hsueh relaxed for the first time that day.

The tavern contained several tables, and the four or five waiters were kept very busy rushing from one to another serving food and wine. Lin Chung and the constables sat for a long time, but no one came to take their order.

Finally, Lin Chung pounded on the table and shouted impatiently, "Ho, tavern keeper, how dare you abuse a customer? You see that I'm a prisoner, so you ignore me! I can pay for what we eat! What's the meaning of this?"

"You don't understand," said the tavern keeper. "My intentions were good."

"You don't sell me wine or meat. What's good-intentioned about that?"

"You don't understand. In our village there's a big landholder called Chai Chin, known in these parts as Lord Chai. In the fraternity of bold men, all address him as Small Whirlwind. He's a descendant of the Chou* dynasty royal family. When the generals surrendered their claims to the throne at Chenchiao, the first Sung emperor bestowed on Chai's ancestors 'The Wrought Iron Pledge.' Since then, no one has dared to molest his family.

"Chai Chin makes a practice of welcoming all bold men. He's always supporting forty or fifty of them in his home. He's left instructions with us at the tavern: 'Tell any prisoner on route to exile to come to my manor. I will help him with money.' If I sold you meat and drink today and you ate until you were red in the face, he would say that you have money and don't need his help. My intentions were good."

Lin Chung turned to the constables. "When I was giving arms instruction to the soldiers in the eastern capital, I often heard military men speak of Lord Chai. So this is where he comes from. Why don't we pay him a call?"

---

*The later Chou dynasty (951-960).

Hsueh Pa and Tung Chao thought it over, then said, "Since we're already here, what have we got to lose?" Collecting their luggage, they asked the tavern keeper, "Where is Lord Chai's manor? We want to visit him."

"Go straight ahead for about three *li* until you cross a big stone bridge. One or two turns, and you'll see a large estate. That's it."

Lin Chung and the constables thanked the tavern keeper and set out. After marching about three *li*, sure enough, they came to a big stone bridge. Crossing to the other side, they found a smooth broad road. In the distance, amid many green willows, they could see the outlines of a manor. A wide moat, flowing around the four sides of the manor, was fringed on both banks by large weeping willow trees. Through the trees, the white outer wall of the stronghold was faintly visible.

After a few more turns down the road, they neared the entrance to the estate. Four or five retainers were sitting on a plank bridge, enjoying the cool of the shade. Approaching the bridge, Lin Chung and the constables bowed to the retainers, and the arms instructor asked:

"Could I trouble you to report to Lord Chai that a prisoner named Lin, on his way to exile from the capital, requests to see him?"

"You're out of luck," said the retainers. "If His Lordship were at home, you'd receive wine and food and money. But he left this morning to go hunting."

"When will he return?"

"Hard to say. Probably he's resting at the eastern manor, but maybe not. We can't tell you for sure."

"Since I'm out of luck, I won't be able to meet him. Let's go back," said Lin Chung to the constables.

Taking leave of the retainers, the three men returned along the same road on which they had come. Lin Chung felt very depressed.

After they had walked more than half a *li*, far off they saw a column of horsemen dash out of a grove and come galloping in the direction of the estate. On a snow-white horse with a curly mane rode a noble-looking gentleman.

He had the brows of a dragon and eyes like a phoenix, with gleaming white teeth and ruby red lips. Drooping moustaches framed his lips; below them was a slim goatee. About thirty-five years of age, he wore a black flowered silk hat with curled up corners, and was dressed in a figured purple gown with designs embroidered on the chest. Around his waist was a handsome tasseled girdle inlaid with precious jade. On his feet were black boots with green stripes and filigreed gold thread. He carried a bow and a quiver of arrows.

Stretching out in a long line, the horsemen raced towards the stronghold.

"Can that be Lord Chai?" Lin Chung wondered. But he didn't dare to ask.

Then he saw the young nobleman turn his white horse out of the column and trot up to him.

"Who is this gentleman wearing the cangue?" the nobleman asked.

Lin quickly bowed and replied, "Your humble servant is called Lin Chung, formerly an arms instructor in the eastern capital's Imperial Guards. Because I offended Marshal Kao, he invented an excuse to send me to the Kaifeng Prefecture and have me sentenced to exile in Tsangchou. We were told at the village tavern that the gallant hero who lives here, Lord Chai, keeps open house for men of talent. But my luck was poor and I was unable to find him."

Leaping from his saddle, the gentleman rushed forward, crying, "I am Chai Chin! A thousand apologies for not being at home to welcome you!" He fell to his knees on the grass and kowtowed.

Lin Chung hastily returned the courtesy. Then the gentleman took him by the hand and led him towards the manor. When the retainers saw them coming, they pushed wide the stronghold gates. Chai Chin led Lin Chung directly to the ceremonial hall, and the two men again exchanged obeisances.

"I have long known of your fame," said Chai Chin. "Who would have thought that today you would come to our humble place. This is one of the happiest events of my life!"

"Your Lordship's name is honoured everywhere. It is revered by all! I never thought that because I was convicted and was passing here on my way to exile I would have the joy of meeting you!"

After much insistence on the part of Chai Chin, Lin Chung took the chair of honour at the table. Hsueh Pa and Tung Chao also were seated. The men who had accompanied Chai Chin on the hunt led their horses into the rear compound and retired. Of them we shall say no more.

Chai Chin ordered his retainers to bring wine. Before long they came with a platter of meat and one of griddle cakes and a pot of warmed wine. Then came another platter heaped with cooked rice; on top of the rice were ten strings of cash.

"These rustics don't recognize a man of quality!" said Chai Chin. "How can they value the arms instructor so lightly? Ho! Take these things back! Bring fine pastries and wine; slaughter a sheep. Be quick!"

"Please, no more, Your Lordship," protested Lin Chung, rising politely. "This is quite enough."

"You mustn't say that! It's a rare privilege to have you here. We can't be remiss in courtesy!"

The retainers soon came rushing in with sweetmeats and wine. Chai Chin stood up and handed out three full goblets. Lin Chung thanked him and drained his cup. The two constables also drank.

"Excuse me a moment, arms instructor," said Chai Chin. Taking off his bow case and quiver of arrows, he went over to the constables and invited them to down a drink with him. Then he seated himself in the host's chair. Lin Chung occupied the chair of the guest of honour; the two constables sat beside him. All chatted idly for a time—of bold adventures and feats of arms.

Before they knew it, the sun had sunk in the west. Wine, food, pastries and delicacies from the sea were set out upon the table before the guests. Toasting each guest personally, Chai Chin drank three rounds. Then he resumed his seat and called: "Bring the soup!"

After the soup was consumed, and six or seven more goblets of wine, a retainer entered and announced: "The teacher has come."

"Good. Invite him to sit with us and meet our guests," said Chai Chin. "Quickly bring another setting."

The new arrival entered and Lin Chung rose to greet him. Cap tilted to one side, arms stiffly belligerent, he swaggered into the hall. "That retainer referred to him as teacher," thought Lin Chung. "He must be His Lordship's arms teacher." Hastily bowing, the arms instructor intoned: "Lin Chung tenders his respects!"

Completely ignoring him, the man did not return his salutation. Lin Chung dared not raise his head. Pointing at Lin Chung, Chai Chin said to the man, whom he called Arms Instructor Hung:

"This is Arms Instructor Lin who teaches the art of spears and staves in the eastern capital's Imperial Guards. You two should know each other."

Lin Chung immediately dropped to his knees and kowtowed.

Arms Instructor Hung said, "Don't kowtow. Get up." He himself didn't even bow.

Observing this, Chai Chin was annoyed. Lin Chung kowtowed twice, then rose and begged Hung to be seated first. Without even a pretence of any courtesy, the fellow promptly took the guest of honour's chair. Chai Chin was quite displeased. Lin Chung slipped into the next seat. The two constables sat down beside him.

"Why is Your Lordship so courteous to an exiled army man?" Arms Instructor Hung asked.

"This gentleman is not an ordinary person. He's an arms instructor in the Eight Hundred Thousand Imperial Guards. How can you regard him lightly, master?"

"Because Your Lordship is fond of feats of arms, these exiled military men are always coming to enjoy your bounty. Anyone who says, 'I'm an arms instructor in spears and staves,' can call at the manor and get food and drink and money and rice. Your Lordship is too gullible!"

Lin Chung said nothing, but Chai Chin retorted, "It's difficult to tell from appearances. You shouldn't underestimate him."

Stung by this last remark, Hung leaped to his feet. "I don't believe him! If he dares to take me on in a bout with staves, then I'll admit he's a genuine arms instructor!"

Chai Chin laughed. "Not a bad idea. Arms Instructor Lin, what do you say?"

"Your humble servant couldn't presume to such a thing," said Lin Chung.

Hung thought to himself, "He doesn't know how to fight, that's sure. He's afraid." And so he was more insistent than ever that Lin Chung accept his challenge.

Chai Chin not only wanted to see an exhibition of Lin's skill, he wanted him to beat Hung and shut the oaf's mouth. "Bring wine," he called. "We'll drink first. The match can wait till the moon is high."

By the time they had consumed another six or seven rounds, the moon had risen and was shining in with such brilliance that the hall was as bright as day. Chai Chin stood up and said, "Arms instructors, please give us a bout."

Lin Chung thought to himself: "This Instructor Hung must be Chai Chin's arms teacher. If I beat him, His Lordship will lose face."

Observing Lin Chung's hesitation, Chai Chin said, "Instructor Hung has not been here long either; no one has taken him on. Please don't refuse, Master Lin. I am most eager to see the skill of you two instructors." Chai Chin said this to indicate that Lin need not have any fears about offending him, and that he should not hold back.

Lin Chung at last felt reassured.

"Come on, come on!" cried Hung, rising. "I'll give you a bout with staves!"

Everyone surged out of the hall into the courtyard. Retainers brought a bundle of wooden staves and laid them on the ground. Hung removed his outer robe and tied up his skirts. Selecting a staff, he struck a fighting pose.

"Come on, come on!" he urged.

"Instructor Lin," said Chai Chin, "please start the bout."

"Don't laugh at my clumsiness, Your Lordship," Lin Chung begged. Choosing a staff, he said to Hung, "Master, please teach me."

Hung glared at him as if wanting to swallow him down in one gulp. Lin Chung advanced holding the staff in both hands. Hung rapped his staff sharply on the ground and rushed at Lin.

After the two arms instructors had fought four or five rounds in the bright moonlight, Lin Chung leaped out of the combat circle. "Halt the bout!" he cried.

"Why won't you show us your skill, instructor?" queried Chai Chin.

"I've lost," said Lin.

"But you haven't fought to a conclusion. How can you say you've lost?"

"If I have to fight with this cangue around my neck, I may just as well consider myself defeated."

"How thoughtless of me," Chai Chin laughed. "That can be remedied easily enough."

He directed his retainers to fetch ten ounces of silver, and when the money was brought he said to the two constables, "May I trouble you to take Lin Chung's cangue off temporarily? If there's any question raised about this when you arrive at the Tsangchou Prison, I will bear all responsibility personally. Divide these ten ounces of silver between you."

Chai Chin looked so lofty and dignified that the constables didn't dare refuse him. Wanting to stay in Chai's good graces, and wanting the ten ounces as well, and since there was no danger of Lin Chung running away, Hsueh Pa removed the wooden collar from his neck.

"Now the two masters can continue their match," said Chai Chin joyfully.

Because Lin's tactics had been cautious, Hung regarded him with scorn. Raising his staff, he prepared to resume combat.

"Just a moment!" Chai Chin exclaimed. He ordered his retainers to bring an ingot of silver weighing twenty-five ounces. In no time at all, the ingot was produced.

"A match between you two instructors is no ordinary contest," said Chai Chin. "Whoever wins gets this silver as a prize." He was hoping in this way to encourage Lin Chung to display his skill. Deliberately, he tossed the ingot on the ground.

Hung was very annoyed that Lin Chung had come, and he coveted the big piece of silver. What's more, he was worried that a defeat would lower his prestige. Vigorously, he struck a fighting pose, then executed an opening flourish called "lifting the torch to sear the heavens."

"His Lordship wants me to defeat him," thought Lin Chung. First holding his staff level, he performed a flourish called "separating the grass to find the snake."

"Come on, come on!" yelled Hung.

He swung his staff downwards. Lin dodged back. Hung pressed forward another pace. Raising his staff, he again chopped down. Lin Chung saw that he was off balance and brought his staff sweeping upwards from the ground. Hung had no time to recover. He tried to twist out of the way, but Lin's staff cracked him hard on the shin bones. Hung dropped his staff and fell heavily.

Delighted, Chai Chin called for wine and presented Lin Chung with a congratulatory goblet. The watchers all laughed. Hung struggled but was unable to rise to his feet. Grinning retainers helped him up. Shame-faced, Hung limped away and left the manor.

Taking Lin Chung by the hand, Chai led him into the rear hall and feasted him with wine. He directed retainers to present Lin with the prize. Lin tried to refuse, but his host insisted, and finally he was compelled to accept.

Chai Chin kept Lin Chung at the manor for several days, entertaining him daily with excellent wines and delicious food. After another six or seven days, since the constables were pressing Lin to leave, Chai gave him a farewell banquet. He also wrote two letters which he handed to the arms instructor, saying:

"The prefect of Tsangchou is a good friend of mine. I'm also on intimate terms with the warden and head keeper of the prison. Give these letters to them and they'll be sure to treat you well."

He presented Lin Chung with another ingot of twenty-five ounces of silver, and bestowed five ounces on the two constables. Then they feasted all night.

Early the next morning, after they had breakfasted, Chai Chin directed a few retainers to go with them and carry their luggage. The cangue was again fastened around Lin Chung's neck. Chai Chin accompanied the party to the manor gate.

"I will send someone with winter clothing for you in a few days," he said to Lin Chung in parting.

"I don't know how to express my gratitude to Your Lordship!" said Lin Chung.

The constables also thanked Chai Chin, then the three departed for Tsangchou. They arrived about noon and sent the luggage bearers back. The constables then went directly to the prefecture and presented their order of exile to an official, who immediately brought Lin Chung before the prefect. Accepting custody of the arms instructor, the prefect issued a receipt of prisoner and wrote out an order committing Lin Chung to prison. The constables, on obtaining the receipt, bade farewell and departed for the eastern capital; of them we shall say no more.

We'll tell of Lin Chung after he was escorted to the prison. Taken into custody, he was placed in a room by himself and directed to wait to be registered. The other prisoners all came to see him.

"The warden and the head keeper here are very bad," they said. "They only want to extort money. If you can bribe them, they'll treat you well. If you have no money, they'll throw you in the dungeon where you'll pray to live and long for death, both in vain! If their palms are greased, you can avoid the hundred blows they give all new prisoners to beat discipline into them. You need only say you're ill and the matter will be postponed indefinitely. Otherwise, it's a hundred strokes that will leave you more dead than alive."

"It's good of you brothers to advise me. If I were to give money, how much would be enough?"

"To do it properly, five ounces of silver for the warden and five for the head keeper would be just about right."

As they were talking, the head keeper came over and asked, "Which one of you is the military man who has been exiled here?"

Lin Chung stepped forward. "I am that humble person."

When the head keeper saw that the arms instructor failed to produce any money, his face darkened. Shaking his finger at Lin, he shouted:

"You bandit! How dare you not kowtow and hail me respectfully when I enter! I heard all about your carryings-on in Kaifeng! Where do you get the gall to behave so insolently in my presence! I can read from the lines on your face that you're destined for nothing but hunger; you'll never rise in the world! What you need is plenty of beatings, you stubborn gaol-bird! For better or worse, you're in my hands now, you felonious wretch! I'll pulverize your bones and pound your flesh to jelly soon enough!"

The keeper cursed vigorously while Lin Chung stood with bowed head. At this storm of invective, the other prisoners fled.

Lin Chung waited until the head keeper had blown off most of his steam, then took out five ounces of silver and handed them to him with a smile. "A trifling gift, brother. Please don't despise it."

"Is this for me and the warden both?"

"Just for you, brother. In addition, here's another ten ounces for the warden. I must trouble you to deliver them to him, brother."

The head keeper grinned broadly. "Arms Instructor Lin, I've heard of your good name before. You're truly a splendid fellow! Marshal Kao has framed you, no doubt about it. Although, for the time being, you're having to suffer this inconvenience, I'm sure you'll eventually make your mark. A man with your reputation and talents never waits around idly for long; one of these days you'll be a big official!"

Lin Chung laughed. "I'm entirely dependant on your kindness."

"You can rest assured," said the head keeper.

Giving him Chai Chin's letters, Lin Chung said, "May I trouble you to deliver these?"

"Letters from Lord Chai? Then you've nothing to worry about. They're worth an ingot of gold each! I'll go and deliver them now. In a little while, the warden will send for you to be registered. When he orders the hundred blows, say that you were ill all during your journey and that you still haven't recovered. I'll speak up for you. We must make it look genuine."

"Many thanks!"

The head keeper took the silver and the letters and departed, leaving Lin Chung alone in the room. The arms instructor sighed.

"'With money you can reach even the gods.' A bitter truth indeed!"

To the warden, the head keeper gave only the five ounces which Lin Chung had originally presented to him. "Lin Chung is an excellent man," he confided. "Here is a letter of introduction from Lord Chai. It seems that Marshal Kao had him exiled on a trumped-up charge. There's nothing much to the whole thing. . . ."

"Since Lord Chai has sent us this letter," said the warden, "we must look after him." He directed that Lin Chung be summoned.

To get back to Lin Chung. He was brooding alone in his room when a turnkey shouted: "The warden orders that new prisoner Lin Chung report to the warden's hall to be registered."

Lin Chung went directly to the hall.

"You are a new prisoner," said the warden. "The first emperor of Sung has bequeathed to us the ancient regulation, 'One hundred blows must be administered to every prisoner newly sent into exile.' Guards! Get him ready!"

"Your humble servant caught a bad cold during his journey here, and still hasn't recovered," said Lin Chung. "I request that the beating be postponed."

"He's not at all well," said the turnkey. "Please have pity on him."

"Since the symptoms of his illness are still evident, perhaps we can put this off for the time being," said the warden. "We can beat him when he regains his health."

"Today, the time is up of that prisoner who has been taking care of the prison temple. Why not let Lin Chung replace him," suggested the head keeper.

The warden promptly wrote out an order and the head keeper accompanied Lin Chung back to his room while he collected his belongings, then led him to the temple.

"I'm being very considerate to you, Arms Instructor Lin, getting you this job," said the head keeper. "It's the easiest work in the prison. All you have to do is burn incense and sweep the floor once in the morning and once again in the evening. You'll soon see that we don't let up on other prisoners from morning till night. As for those without money, we throw them into the dungeon where they pray to live and long for death, both in vain!"

"Thanks for your protection," said Lin Chung. He gave the head keeper another few ounces of silver. "There's one more matter I must trouble you about, brother. Could you have this cangue taken from my neck?"

"Just leave it to me," said the head keeper as he tucked the money away. He hurried to the warden and relayed the plea. The cangue was removed.

From then on, Lin Chung slept and ate in the temple. Every day, he did nothing except burn incense and sweep the floor. Before he knew it, forty or fifty days had gone by. The warden and the head keeper, having been bribed, were always very cordial. He was left free to come and go as he pleased, with no restrictions. Lord Chai sent a man with money and winter clothing for him. All the prisoners became recipients of Lin Chung's charity.

To make a long story short, one day around noon as winter

was drawing near, Lin Chung was strolling outside the prison gates. Suddenly, he heard someone behind him call:

"Arms Instructor Lin, what are you doing here?"

Lin Chung turned around and looked.

And as a result of seeing the man who hailed him: Fire and flames nearly put an end to his life; out in the wind and snow he narrowly escaped suffering mortal wounds.

Who was the man whom Lin Chung saw? If you want to know, listen to our next episode.

Lin Chung Shelters from the Snowstorm in the Mountain Spirit Temple Lu Chien Sets Fire to the Fodder Depot

As we were saying, Lin Chung was strolling along, when someone behind him called his name. Turning around, he saw the tavern waiter Li Hsiao-erh. When they first became acquainted in Kaifeng, the eastern capital, Lin had helped him financially several times. Later, Hsiao-erh stole money from the tavern keeper and was arrested. He was going to be sent to the prefect but Lin Chung spoke up in his behalf, and he did not have to stand trial. Lin also paid back the money for him and he was released. Although Hsiao-erh could no longer find work in the capital, thanks to the travelling expenses which Lin gave him, he was able to leave Kaifeng and seek employment elsewhere. Today, unexpectedly, they met again in Tsangchou.

"What are you doing here, Brother Hsiao-erh?" asked Lin Chung.

Hsiao-erh kowtowed and replied, "After you saved me, benefactor, and gave me travelling money, I looked everywhere for a job, but in vain. Finally, I wandered into Tsangchou. Here, a tavern keeper named Wang took me on as his assistant. Because I was a hard worker, and could make tasty dishes and sauces, the customers all praised me and business improved. The tavern keeper had a daughter, and he gave her to me in marriage. Now, both he and my mother-in-law are dead. Only my wife and I are left. We run a tavern in front of the prison. I was just passing by on my way to collect some bills. What are you doing here, benefactor?"

Lin pointed to the mark on his face. "Because I crossed the will of Marshal Kao, he conspired against me and had me convicted and exiled to this place. At present, I look after the prison temple. I don't know what they'll do with me in the future. I never expected to meet you here."

Hsiao-erh brought Lin Chung to his home, invited him to be seated, and called his wife in to kowtow. Both husband and wife said happily, "We have no close relatives. Your coming here today, benefactor, is like a gift from heaven."

"I'm a prisoner," said Lin. "Won't associating with me sully your name?"

"How can you talk like that!" said Hsiao-erh. "Everyone knows your excellent reputation! Be sure to bring all your washing and mending to my wife."

He entertained Lin Chung with food and drink, and that night saw him back to the prison temple. The following morning, he came again to invite Lin to his home.

From then on, Hsiao-erh and Lin called on each other frequently. Hsiao-erh often sent tea or soup to Lin in the prison. Moved by the couple's respect and devotion, Lin gave them money from time to time to use in their business.

To skip the idle chatter, time passed quickly. Winter came. All of Lin Chung's padded winter garments were stitched and mended by Hsiao-erh's wife. On day, while Hsiao-erh was cooking in the entry, a man slipped in and sat down inside at one of the tables. Then another fellow furtively entered. The first man was an army officer, by the looks of him. The second seemed more like an attendant. He also hurried in and sat down.

Hsiao-erh went up to them. "Wine?" he queried.

The officer handed Hsiao-erh an ounce of silver. "Take this on account. Bring us three or four jugs of good wine.

When our guests come, serve some food and tidbits. You choose the dishes. You needn't ask me."

"You've invited guests, sir?"

"I must trouble you to go to the prison and invite the warden and the head keeper here for a chat. If they question you, just say, 'A gentleman requests that you come and discuss certain matters. He is looking forward to your arrival.' "

Hsiao-erh assented and left. At the prison, he first relayed the request to the head keeper then, together, they extended the invitation to the warden, after which all three went to the tavern. The gentleman, the warden and the head keeper exchanged greetings.

"We haven't met before," said the warden. "May we ask your name, sir?"

"I have a letter of introduction here, which I will give you shortly," replied the man. "But first let's have some wine!"

Hsiao-erh quickly opened the jugs and served the food and pastries. The gentleman called for a ceremonial tray of wine goblets and, after filling and handing them out, invited his guests to be seated. Hsiao-erh dashed back and forth like a shuttle, serving without cease. The gentleman's attendant took care of the warming of the wine. After several score rounds had been drunk, more tidbits to go with the wine were ordered.

"My attendant will warm the wine," the gentleman said to Hsiao-erh. "You needn't come in for a while. We want to talk privately."

Hsiao-erh said, "Very well, sir," and left the room. Outside the door, he conferred with his wife.

"There's something fishy about those two."

"What do you mean?"

"They've both got Kaifeng accents and neither of them knows the warden. When I went in with those tidbits just now, I heard the head keeper murmur something about 'Marshal Kao.' Wasn't he the one who harmed Instructor Lin? I'll stay here at the door and keep an eye on them. You go and listen on the other side of the partition wall."

"Why not bring Instructor Lin here from the prison and see if he recognizes them?"

"You don't know what a terrible temper he has. He's liable to commit murder and burn the place down. If I called him and that gentleman turned out to be the Steward Lu he mentioned the other day, Lin would never let him escape alive. If anything happened here, you and I would be involved. You'd better go and listen. We'll decide what to do later."

"Very well," said the wife. She went and listened for a time. Then she returned and said:

"They're whispering with their heads together and I couldn't hear much. But I saw that fellow who looks like an officer take something wrapped in a white cloth from his attendant and give it to the warden and head keeper. Maybe there's money in it. I heard the head keeper say, 'Leave everything to us. We'll put an end to him, come what may.' "

Just then, from the inner room a voice shouted, "Bring the soup!" Hsiao-erh hastened to comply. As he entered, he saw that the warden had a letter in his hand. Hsiao-erh served the soup, then brought some more dishes of food.

The guests again feasted. After the bill was paid, the warden and head keeper first departed. The other two, heads stealthily lowered, then also left.

Shortly afterwards, Lin Chung entered the tavern. "Brother Hsiao-erh," he said, "I hope you're prospering!"

"Please sit down, benefactor," Hsiao-erh begged hastily. "I was just about to look for you. I must tell you something very important."

"What is it?" asked Lin Chung.

Hsiao-erh led him to the inner room, invited him to be seated, and said, "A little while ago a couple of fishy looking fellows from the eastern capital came to the tavern and invited the warden and the head keeper to join them. They ate and drank for a long time. I overheard the head keeper say something about 'Marshal Kao' and I got suspicious and told my wife to listen in on their conversation. They were talking softly with their heads close together and she couldn't hear anything. She was about to give up when she heard the head keeper say, 'Leave everything to us. We'll finish him off, come what may!' The other two handed the warden and head keeper a package of money. They drank some more and then left. I don't know who these fellows are, but I don't trust them. I'm afraid they want to harm you, benefactor."

"What do they look like?" asked Lin.

"One is of average build, fair, clean shaven, about thirty or so. The other fellow isn't very tall either. He has a ruddy complexion."

Startled, Lin Chung cried, "That man of thirty must be Steward Lu. The filthy thief, how dare he come here to harm me! If I get hold of him I'll smash him to a jelly!"

"The main thing is to be on your guard," said Hsiao-erh. " 'Take care not to choke when you eat or trip when you walk,' as the old saying goes."

Lin Chung left Hsiao-erh's home in a towering rage. On the street, he bought a sharp dagger. Carrying it on his person, he made a search of all the streets and lanes. Hsiao-erh and his wife were in a cold sweat. But that night nothing happened.

At daybreak the following morning, Lin rose, washed his face and rinsed his mouth, then took up the dagger and again prowled through all the streets and lanes both in the city and on the outskirts. He patrolled all day, even searching the prison, but nothing was stirring. Returning to Hsiao-erh's place, he said:

"Nothing happened today either."

"Benefactor," said Hsiao-erh, "let's hope it stays that way. But remain on your guard."

Lin went back to the prison temple, where he spent the night. He walked the streets for four or five days, without success. His temper gradually began to cool.

On the sixth day, the warden summoned Lin Chung into his hall and said, "You've been here for some time now. For the sake of Lord Chai's prestige, we must improve your lot. Fifteen *li* outside the city's east gate is a large army fodder depot. Every month you can collect some fees from the people delivering the fodder. An old army man is in charge there. I've decided to give you the job and have him replace you in the prison temple. Out at the depot, you'll be able to earn a little spending money. Go there with the head keeper and take over."

"I'll do that, sir," said Lin.

He first left the prison and went directly to Hsiao-erh's house. Lin told the couple the news.

"Today, the warden is sending me to take charge of the army fodder depot. What do you think?"

"It's a better job than the prison temple," replied Hsiao-erh. "You can earn some regular fees out there. Usually, no one gets that post without paying a bribe."

"Not only haven't they harmed me, but they've given me this good job instead. I don't know what to make of it. . . ."

"Why be suspicious, benefactor? As long as nothing happens, that's fine. The only trouble is you'll be living quite far from us. After a while, I'll come and see you, if I have time." Hsiao-erh pressed Lin Chung to join him in several rounds of drinks.

To make a long story short, the two separated and Lin Chung returned to the prison temple. He packed his belongings, put his dagger in his belt, took up a spear and set out with the head keeper for the fodder depot.

It was a bitterly cold winter day. The sky was overcast, and they walked in the teeth of a rising wind amid thickly swirling snowflakes. Since there was no place along the road to buy drinks, Lin and the keeper soon reached the depot.

Surrounded by an earthen wall, the depot had a gate with two doors. They pushed the doors open and entered the compound. They saw a thatched building of seven or eight sections, which was serving as a storehouse for fodder. All around were piles of hay. In the centre stood a small thatched shack. Inside, they found the old soldier huddle over a fire.

"This is Lin Chung," the head keeper said to him. "The warden has sent him to replace you. You are to go back to take care of the prison temple. You can hand over your duties."

The old soldier gave Lin Chung the keys and said, "The stuff in the storehouse is under official seal. And those haystacks there are all numbered."

After he took Lin around and counted the stacks, the old soldier brought him back to the shack and gathered his belongings. As he was leaving, he said, "I'll give you my brazier, my pot, my bowl and my dish."

"I have such things in the temple too," said Lin. "You can have mine."

The old soldier pointed to a gourd bottle hanging on the wall. He said, "If you want to buy wine, there's a little market two or three *li* east down the road." Then he and the head keeper departed for the prison.

As to Lin Chung, he placed his bundle and bedding on the brick bed and lighted a fire in the stove underneath. There was some charcoal in the room, and Lin added a few sticks. Then he looked around the shack. Very dilapidated, it shook with every gust of wind.

"How can I pass the winter here?" thought Lin. "When the storm stops I must bring a mason out from the city to repair this place."

Although he hugged the fire, he still felt cold. "The old soldier said there was a little market two *li* from here," he recalled. "Why don't I go and buy some wine?"

He took some money from his bundle, tied the gourd bottle to the end of his spear, covered the stove opening, put on his broad-brimmed felt hat, took the keys and shut the door of the shack behind him. Coming through the compound gate, he closed and locked it. Then, carrying the keys, he headed east. The snow-covered ground was a mass of tiny white jade flakes. Lin Chung trudged forward with the north wind on his back. It was snowing very hard.

He had gone less than half a *li* when he observed an ancient temple. Pressing his palms together before his forehead and bowing, Lin Chung said, "May the gods protect me. I must come here one of these days and burn some paper money in sacrifice."

Lin continued on his way. Ahead, he saw a cluster of houses. He halted, and peered through the storm. The buildings were enclosed by a fence. A clump of broom grass was hanging outside one of them. Knowing that this must be a tavern, Lin went inside.

"Where are you from, sir?" the tavern keeper asked.

"Do you recognize this gourd bottle?" Lin Chung countered.

The man looked at it and said, "It belongs to the old soldier at the fodder depot."

"That's right," said Lin.

"So you're the new custodian," said the man. "Please be seated, brother. It's a bitterly cold day. Let me treat you to a few goblets, by way of welcome."

The keeper served a platter of sliced beef, heated a pot of wine and invited Lin to help himself. Lin bought some more beef, drank a few cups, then had the gourd filled with wine. Wrapping up the two orders of beef, he left a few pieces of silver, tied the gourd bottle to the end of his spear and placed the beef inside his shirt.

"Thanks for your trouble," said Lin. He went out through the fence gate and started back against the wind. Now that night had come, the snow was falling harder than ever.

Plodding through the snow in the teeth of the north wind, Lin Chung hurried back to the fodder depot. When he unlocked the doors and entered the compound, he uttered a cry of dismay. Actually, the gods who see everything and protect the good and virtuous were saving Lin Chung's life with that snowstorm. The thatched shack had collapsed under the weight of the snow.

"What am I going to do?" Lin wondered.

He put his spear and gourd down in the snow. Worried that the embers in the brazier might set the place on fire, he pulled open a section of the wall of the fallen shack, pushed himself halfway in and felt around. But the embers had been extinguished by the melted snow. Groping with his hand on the brick bed, Lin found his quilt and pulled it out, emerging again into the dark night.

"I've no place to build a fire," he pondered. "How am I going to manage?" Then he remembered the ancient temple, half a *li* down the road. "I can spend the night there," he thought. "When daylight comes, I'll decide what to do next."

He rolled up his quilt, shouldered his spear with the wine gourd dangling from one end, closed the compound doors once more, locked them, and proceeded to the temple. Entering, he shut the door and propped against it a big stone which he had noticed lying to one side. Walking further into the temple, he saw on a platform an idol of a mountain spirit with golden armour, flanked by a nether region judge and a small demon, one on each side. In a corner was a pile of paper. Lin Chung inspected the whole temple but could find neither neighbours nor anyone in charge.

Lin placed his spear and gourd bottle on the pile of paper and untied his quilt. He removed his broad-brimmed felt hat, shook the snow from his clothes and peeled off his white tunic which was half soaked, then put it together with his hat on the altar table. Covering himself to the waist with the quilt, he drank from the gourd bottle from time to time, helping the cold wine down with slices of the beef he had been carrying.

As he was eating, he heard a loud crackling outside. Leaping to his feet, he peered through a crack and saw that the fodder depot was in flames and burning fiercely. Lin grabbed his spear. He was about to open the door and dash to the fire when he heard men's voices. Leaning against the door, he listened. The footsteps of three men came directly to the temple.

The men pushed the temple door with their hands, but the big stone held the door fast and they couldn't open it. They stood under the eaves watching the fire. One of them said:

"Not a bad plan, eh?"

"We're much indebted to the warden and to you, head keeper," someone replied. "When I return to the capital and report to the Marshal, he undoubtedly will make you both big officials. Now Arms Instructor Chang has no excuse to refuse."

"We've taken care of Lin Chung properly this time!" said a third. "Young Master Kao is sure to recover!"

"We tried to arrange the match three or four times," said a voice. "We told that lout Chang, 'Your son-in-law is dead,' but he wouldn't believe it. Young Master Kao's ailment kept getting worse. And so the Marshal sent us specially to beg you two gentlemen to help. Today, we've succeeded at last!"

"I climbed over the wall and set a score of haystacks afire. I'd like to see him get away!"

"The depot is almost completely destroyed."

"Even if he escapes with his life, burning down a military fodder depot is a crime punishable by death!"

"Let's go back to the city."

"Wait a little longer. If we bring a couple of his bones with us to the capital, the Marshal and the Young Master will praise us for doing the job thoroughly."

Lin Chung recognized them by their voices. One was the head keeper, another was the steward Lu Chien, the third was Fu An. "Heaven took pity on me," thought Lin. "If that thatched shack hadn't collapsed, I'll have been roasted to death by these villains!"

Softly, he pulled the stone away from the door. Clutching his spear, Lin Chung pushed open the door with his left hand and roared:

"Where do you think you're going, knaves!"

The three, who had just been leaving, froze, too shocked to move.

Raising his hand, Lin speared the head keeper to the ground.

"Spare me!" cried Steward Lu, weak with terror.

Fu An had run only a score of paces when Lin Chung caught up. With one thrust, Lin plunged the spear into his back, and he also fell.

As Lin turned, he saw Steward Lu starting to flee. Before Lu had gone three paces, Lin Chung shouted, "Halt, treacherous thief!" He grabbed Lu by the front of his tunic and threw him flat on his back in the snow.

Lin jabbed his spear into the ground, put one foot on Lu's chest, whipped out his dagger and held it against the steward's face.

"Filthy wretch!" he grated. "I never wronged you; how can you have injured me so! Truly, 'Killing can be forgiven, but never betrayal!' "

"This wasn't my idea," Lu pleaded. "The Marshal ordered me to do it! I didn't dare refuse!"

"Treacherous knave!" cried Lin. "We were friends since childhood, yet today you come to destroy me! How can you excuse yourself! Have a taste of this knife!"

He ripped open Lu's clothes, stabbed the blade into his heart and twisted. As blood spurted everywhere, Lin tore out his heart and liver.

Turning his head, Lin saw the head keeper struggling to his feet to run. Lin seized him in a flash. "Now I know what an evil scoundrel you are!" he shouted. "Take that!" He cut off the keeper's head and tied it to the end of his spear.

Next, he went back to Fu An and Lu Chien and cut off their heads too. He put away his knife, tied the three heads together by the hair, carried them into the temple and placed them on the altar in front of the mountain spirit idol. Then he put on his white tunic, tied his waist sash, clapped the broad-brimmed felt hat on his head and finished off the cold wine in the gourd bottle.

Tossing his quilt and the bottle aside, Lin took up his spear, left the temple and started east. He had gone only four or five *li* when he saw people from a neighbouring village hastening with water buckets and pikes to put out the blaze.

"Hurry and save the place!" Lin Chung called to them. "I'm going to report the fire to the officials!"

Spear in hand, he walked on rapidly.

Red-haired Devil Lies Drunk in Lingkuan Temple;
Chao the Heavenly King Acknowledges a "Nephew"
in East-bank Village

As I was saying, when Lei Heng entered Lingkuan Temple he saw this big fellow sleeping on the altar. The soldiers rushed forward, tied him up, and dragged him outside. It was only about the fifth watch – the sun had not yet risen. Lei Heng said: "Let's take the lout to the manor of Ward Chief Chao. We can get some breakfast there, then we'll turn him over to the county

magistrate for questioning." The company proceeded rapidly to the manor.

The ward chief of East-bank Village was surnamed Chao, his given name was Kai. Born of a well-to-do family native to these parts for many generations, Chao had always fought injustice and helped the needy. He liked nothing better than befriending gallant men, and put them up in his manor whenever they came to him, no matter what the circumstances. When they were ready to go, he gave them silver for travelling expenses. Extremely fond of play with weapons, Chao was very strong. He had never married and practised body-building exercises from morning till night.

Outside the East Gate of Yuncheng, the county seat, were two villages which the county administered. Separated by a large stream, one was called East-bank, the other West-bank. Formerly evil spirits had haunted West-bank. They lured people into the stream in broad daylight, laying in wait beneath the waters. No one could cope with them. One day a monk came by, and the villagers told him all about it. Pointing to a place, the monk instructed them to build a pagoda there of black stone; this would repress evil on the bank of the stream. The result was the spirits left the village of West-bank and moved over to East-bank.

When Chao Kai learned of this he was furious. Wading the stream, he picked up the black stone pagoda, carried it across single-handed and deposited it on the East-bank. From then on he was famed as Chao Kai, the Tower-shifting Heavenly King. He became the undisputed ruler of the village, and gallant men everywhere knew his name.

That morning Lei Heng and his soldiers took the big fellow to the manor and knocked on the gate. When the retainers found out who was calling, they reported to the ward chief. Chao Kai was still in bed, but hearing that Constable Lei had come, he ordered that the gate be opened immediately. The retainers complied. After the soldiers suspended the big fellow from a rafter in the gate house, Lei Heng took ten or so of their leaders to a thatched hall and sat down.

Chao Kai, who had left his bed to greet them, asked: "What business brings you here, constable?"

"On orders of his honour the magistrate, Chu Tung and I have led two patrols into the countryside to look for bandits," said Lei Heng. "Now we're tired and want to rest a while, so we've come to your manor. I hope we're not disturbing you."

"Not at all," replied Chao Kai. He told his retainers to prepare food and drink, and first to bring some tea. "Did you catch any thieves in our village?" he queried.

"Just now we discovered a big fellow sleeping in that Lingkuan Temple out front. I could see he was no gentleman. He evidently got drunk and fell asleep in there. So we tied him up. I was going to take him to the county magistrate straight away, but in the first place it was too early, and in the second place I wanted to inform you, ward chief. In case the magistrate asks you about it in the future, you'll be able to answer. I have the prisoner hung up in your gate house."

Chao Kai made a mental note of this. "Thank you for telling me, constable," he replied. A short time later, his retainers brought in wine and platters of food. Chao Kai said: "Talking out here is not very convenient. Let's sit inside." Ordering a retainer to light a lamp, he conducted Lei Heng to the porch of a rear building.

After they had both taken their places at a table – Chao Kai in the host's seat, Lei Heng in the guest's – a few retainers carried in platters of tidbits, while another poured the wine. Chao Kai ordered that wine also be given to the soldiers. The retainers led the soldiers to an esplanade and treated them as guests, serving large platters of meat and big bowls of wine, and urging them to eat their fill.

As he courteously plied the constable with food and drink, Chao Kai thought to himself: "What thief could he have caught in our village? I must have a look." After downing six or seven goblets of wine with Lei Heng, he summoned one of his stewards and said: "Keep the constable company. I'm going out to relieve myself. I'll be back shortly."

While the steward drank with Lei Heng, Chao Kai got a lantern and went directly to the main gate. None of the soldiers was around. All were inside, drinking. Chao Kai asked one of his retainers, who was guarding the gate: "That robber the constable caught — where have they got him tied?"

"He's locked in gate house," said the retainer.

Chao Kai pushed open the door and looked. The fellow was suspended high above the floor. His body was a mass of swarthy flesh, his dangling legs were black and hairy, his feet were bare. Chao Kai shone his lantern on the man's face. It was ruddy and broad. On the side of his temple was a scarlet birthmark from which reddish-brown hair sprouted.

"Where are you from, young fellow?" Chao Kai asked him. "I haven't seen you in our village before."

"Your servant is a stranger from a distant township. I came to offer my services to a man, but they've arrested me as a thief. I must get justice."

"Who did you want to join in this village?"

"A gallant man."

"His name?"

"He's called Ward Chief Chao."

"Why did you want to see him?"

"Chao Kai is famed everywhere as a champion of righteousness. There's a rare chance for riches I'd like to tell him about."

"Seek no further. I am Ward Chief Chao. If you want me to save you, pretend to recognize me as your mother's brother. In a little while when I come here to see off Constable Lei and his men, call me 'Uncle.' I will address you as 'Nephew.' I'll say that you were four or five when you left here. That's why I didn't recognize you when you came again, looking for me."

"If you can rescue me, I'll be deeply grateful," said the young man. "Please help me, champion!"

Carrying his lantern, Chao Kai left the gate house. He again barred the door, then hurried back to the building in the rear.

"Forgive me for neglecting you," he said to Lei Heng.

"I'm putting you to too much trouble," the constable replied. "It's really not right."

They drank several cups of wine together. Soon light began shining in through the window.

"It's brightening in the east," said Lei Heng. "Your servant must take his leave. I have to sign in at the county office."

"You have your official duties, constable. I dare not detain you. If business brings you to our humble village again, be sure to call on me."

"I certainly will pay my respects, ward chief. Please don't bother to see me off."

"At least let me escort you to the manor gate."

Chao Kai and Lei Heng emerged from the building. The soldiers, who had dined well, now took up their spears and staves and proceeded to the gate house. There they let down the young man they had suspended and led him out through the door, his hands tied behind his back.

"He's a big fellow!" Chao Kai remarked.

"That rogue is the thief we caught in Lingkuan Temple," said Lei Heng. Even before he had finished speaking, the young man shouted:

"Uncle, save me!"

Chao Kai pretended to peer at him. Then he cried: "Why, isn't that rascal Wang the Third?"

"Yes, it's me, uncle. Save me!"

Everyone was astonished. "Who is he?" Lei Heng asked Chao Kai. "How does he know you, ward chief?"

"He's my sister's son, Wang the Third. Why was the scamp resting in the temple? He lived here till he was four or five, then my sister and her husband moved to the Southern Capital. I didn't see him for ten years. He came again when he was about fifteen, accompanying a merchant from the city on a business trip. That was the last I saw of him. I've heard many people say the scoundrel is no good. What's he doing here? I'd never have recognized him if it weren't for that scarlet birthmark on the side of his temple."

"Little Third," he shouted at the young man, "why didn't you come to me directly? Why did you go into the village and steal?"

"But uncle, I didn't steal anything!" the young fellow protested.

"If you're not a thief, why have they brought you here?" Chao Kai demanded. Snatching a stave from one of the soldiers, he belaboured the young man about the head.

"Don't beat him," Lei Heng and the others urged. "Let's hear what he has to say."

"Uncle, don't be angry," said the young fellow. "Let me speak. Since the last time I came at the age of fifteen, ten years have gone by, isn't that so? Last night on the road I had one cup of wine too many. I didn't dare call on you drunk, so I went to the temple to sleep it off, first. How did I know they were going to nab me without a word? I'm not a thief!"

Chao Kai again rushed at him with the stave. "Animal!" he cried. "Instead of coming to me directly, you guzzled yourself full of yellow wine on the road! Couldn't you get all you want in my home? You've disgraced me!"

"Calm yourself, ward chief. Your nephew isn't a thief," Lei Heng said soothingly. "I got suspicious, finding a big fellow like him asleep in the temple. After all, I'd never seen him before. So I arrested him and brought him here. I would never have done it had I known he was your nephew."

Lei Heng ordered his soldiers to untie the young fellow and turn him over to the ward chief. They at once did so. "Please don't take it amiss," the constable pleaded. "Had I known he was your nephew, this wouldn't have happened. I hope you're not offended. We must go back, now."

"Just a moment, constable," said Chao Kai. "Please come into my small manor. I've something to say."

Lei Heng returned with the ward chief to the thatched building. Chao Kai handed him ten ounces of silver. "Just a paltry gift, constable," Chao Kai said. "Please don't score it for being so small."

"But you shouldn't be doing this!"

"If you don't accept, I'll know you're displeased with me."

"Since you're so generous, ward chief, I can't refuse. Some day I'll show my gratitude."

Chao Kai instructed the young man to thank Lei Heng. Then he distributed pieces of silver among the soldiers and saw the company to the manor gate. Lei Heng bade the ward chief farewell and departed with his men.

Chao Kai took the young man to the rear building and gave him clothes and a hat. He asked his name and place of origin.

"Your servant's family name is Liu; his given name is Tang. My ancestral home is in the East Luchow Region. Because of this scarlet birthmark on the side of my temple, since childhood I've been known as the 'Red-haired Devil.' I've made this trip especially to inform you of a rare chance for riches, brother ward chief. Last night I fell asleep, drunk, in the temple, and those oafs nabbed me and tied me up. Fortunately, today, I've met you at last. Please be seated, brother, and accept my four kowtows."

When the young man had completed his obeisances, Chao Kai said: "You say you have a rare chance to tell me about. What is it?"

"Ever since childhood, your servant has drifted about. I've been to many places and made friends with many gallant men. Though I've often heard them speak of you, brother, I never thought I'd have occasion to seek you out. I've also met merchants from east of the mountains and north of the river who've served under you, brother. That's why I'm willing to tell you this. If there are no outsiders around, I'd like to put the whole thing before you frankly."

"You can speak freely. Only my most trusted men are here."

"It's said that Governor Liang of Taming, the Northern Capital, has bought jewels and art objects worth a hundred thousand strings of cash to send to his father-in-law Premier Tsai in the Eastern Capital as birthday gifts. Last year he also sent birthday gifts of the same value. But they were seized by unknown persons along the way; to this day the robbers haven't been caught. This year Governor Liang has bought another hundred thousand strings worth of jewels and art objects. The route by which they'll be sent has already been chosen. They must be delivered before Premier Tsai's birthday on the fifteenth of the sixth lunar month. In my humble opinion these things were purchased with unclean money; there will be nothing wrong in taking them. We've only to work out a plan for capturing them along the way. Heaven knows it will be no crime. I've often heard that you're a real man, brother, and that you have a remarkable skill with weapons. Although I'm not very talented, I know a little about them myself. Not only can I deal with four or five men at a time, but if I had my spear I wouldn't be afraid even if two thousand men on horseback came at me together. If you don't despise me, brother, I'm more than willing to lend a hand. What do you think of the idea?"

"Excellent! We must plan carefully. But you've just come, and you've been rather battered about. Why not rest a while in the guest house? Let me give the matter some thought. We'll talk more about it later."

Chao Kai ordered a retainer to lead Liu Tang to the guest house. The retainer did so, then went off.

"I certainly was having a hard time," Liu Tang thought to himself. "It's lucky Chao Kai was able to get me out of that scrape. That lout Lei Heng grabbed me for a thief in broad daylight and suspended me all night from a rafter! The villain can't have travelled very far. Why not take a weapon and go after him? I can knock down all those rascals, bring Chao Kai back his silver, and work off some of my anger at the same time. A great idea!"

Liu Tang came out of the house, took a sword from the rack and left the manor. As he strode south, the sky was already light. Soon he could see the constable and his soldiers marching slowly ahead. Hurrying after them, Liu Tang cried: "Constable, stand where you are!"

Startled, Lei Heng turned to see Liu Tang advancing towards him rapidly, sword in hand. Lei hastily took a sword from one of his soldiers.

"What do you want, varlet?" he shouted.

"If you know what's good for you, you'll give me those ten ounces of silver. Then maybe I'll forgive you!"

"Your uncle presented me with that money. What is it to you? If it weren't for his sake, I'd end your knavish life! What gall to demand my silver!"

"I'm no thief, but you suspended me from a rafter all night and swindled my uncle out of ten ounces of silver to boot! Return it to me, if you've got any sense, and I'll let you off. If you don't, I'll spill your blood on the spot!"

Furious, Lei Heng pointed his finger at Liu Tang and swore: "Worthless lying thief! You're a disgrace to your family! Impertinent dog!"

"Dirty extortioner of the people! You dare to curse me?"

"You're a bandit to the marrow of your bones! Leave Chao Kai out of this! You're a bandit, heart and liver! Don't think you can pull that sort of thing on me!"

"I'm going to settle this with you once and for all!" Brandishing his sword, the enraged Liu Tang charged towards Lei Heng.

The constable raised his own sword with a laugh and strode forward to meet him. They clashed in the middle of the road and fought over fifty rounds, with neither vanquishing the other.

When the soldiers saw that Lei Heng couldn't defeat Liu Tang, they began closing in on the young man. But just then the fence gate of a nearby house opened and a man holding a length of chain in each hand emerged, crying: "You two bold men there — desist! I've been watching a long time. Rest a moment. I've something to say." He swung the chains between the contestants. Both lowered their swords, jumped out of the combat circle, and waited.

The man had the appearance of a scholar. He wore a cylindrical-shaped hat that came down almost to his eyebrows, and a wide flaxen gown with a black border that was gathered at the waist by a tea-coloured sash. His feet were clad in white socks and silk shoes. His handsome and refined face was adorned with a long beard. This was Wu Yung the Wizard. His alternate name was Hsueh-chiu. His Taoist appellation was Master Increasing Light. Since the earliest times his family had resided in this village.

Chain in hand, Wu Yung pointed at Liu Tang and said: "Stay where you are, young man. Why are you fighting with the constable?"

Liu Tang glared at him. "None of your business, scholar!"

"I'll tell you why, teacher," said Lei Heng. "Last night we caught this rogue sleeping naked in the Lingkuan Temple and brought him to Ward Chief Chao's manor. When we discovered that he was the ward chief's nephew, we released him for his uncle's sake. The ward chief invited us to have some wine and presented me with a gift. Unknown to his uncle, this scoundrel

chased after us and demanded that I return the gift to him. How do you like that for nerve?"

"I've known Chao Kai ever since we were children," Wu Yung thought to himself. "He's often discussed his private affairs with me, and I'm familiar with all of his relatives. But I've never heard of this nephew. Besides, he's the wrong age. There's something fishy here. I've got to stop this fight, first. Then I can question him."

"Don't be so stubborn, big fellow," he said to the young man. "Your uncle and I are friends. I know that he's on good terms with this constable. If you take back the little gift he's given him, it will make your uncle look bad. Have some respect for me. I'll talk this over with your uncle later."

"Scholar, you don't know the facts," said Liu Tang. "My uncle didn't give the gift willingly. The rogue extorted that silver out of him! If he doesn't return it to me, I swear I'm not going back!"

"I'll return it only if the ward chief himself asks for it," said Lei Heng. "I won't give it to you!"

"You slandered me and said I was a thief. You extorted my uncle's silver. How can you refuse to return it?"

"It's not your silver! I won't return it! I won't! I won't!"

"You'll have to ask this sword in my hand whether you'll return it or not!"

"You two have already fought for a long time without either of you winning," said Wu Yung. "How much longer do you intend to fight?"

"If he doesn't return that silver, I'll fight him until only one of us is left alive!" cried Liu Tang.

"If I were afraid of you, I could have had one of my soldiers help me," Lei Heng shouted angrily. "But I'm too much of a man for that. I'm going to knock you head over heels all by myself!"

Liu Tang thumped his chest furiously. "Let's see you do it!" He came at him.

The constable also advanced, brandishing his arms and stamping his feet. Both men were spoiling to resume the fight. Wu Yung thrust himself between them, but his admonitions were in vain. Liu Tang waved his sword, just waiting for a chance to attack. Lei Heng, cursing the young fellow for ten thousand kinds of a thief, also held his sword at the ready. It was then that the soldiers exclaimed:

"Here comes the ward chief."

Liu Tang turned and looked. He saw Chao Kai, his unfastened tunic draped over his shoulders, running down the road. "Behave yourself, you young whelp!" shouted Chao Kai.

Wu Yung smiled. "Thank Heaven the ward chief has come. He's the only one who can stop them."

Chao Kai rushed up, panting. "Why are you two fighting?"

"Your nephew chased after me, sword in hand, and demanded my silver," replied Lei Heng. "I said: 'I won't give it to you. I'll return it only to the ward chief himself. This has nothing to do with you.' He fought me fifty rounds, then this teacher came and stopped us."

"That young animal!" said Chao Kai. "I didn't know anything about it. For my sake, constable, please continue on your way. I'll call on you another day and make my apologies."

"I knew the young rascal was talking rot," said Lei Heng. "I didn't take him seriously. I'm sorry you've had to come all this distance." He bade the ward chief farewell and departed. We'll say no more of him.

Then Wu Yung confided to Chao Kai: "It's lucky you arrived when you did, or something serious might have happened. That nephew of yours is remarkable! A splendid swordsman! I was watching from inside the fence. The famed duellist Lei Heng couldn't touch him. Lei Heng was on the defensive all the time. If they had gone another few rounds, he surely would have lost his life. That's why I hurried out to stop them. Where is your nephew from? I've never seen him at your manor."

"I was just about to send a messenger to invite you over to my humble home for a talk, when I noticed that Liu Tang was gone and a sword was missing from the rack," said Chao Kai. "A little cowherd told me he had seen a big fellow, carrying a sword, running south. I hastily followed. Fortunately, you had already stopped the fight. Please come to my humble manor. There's a matter on which I need your advice."

Wu Yung first returned to his quarters and hung up the chains in his study. He said to his landlord: "When my students come, say that their teacher is busy today. Tell them they can take the day off." He closed his door and locked it, then proceeded with Chao Kai and Liu Tang to the ward chief's manor.

Chao Kai led them directly to an inner room in the rear building, where they took appropriate seats as host and guests.

"Ward chief, who is this person?" Wu Yung asked.

"A bold fellow in the fraternity of gallant men, Liu Tang, from a family in the East Luchow Region. He came especially to inform me of a rare chance for riches. Last night he fell asleep, drunk, in the Lingkuan Temple, and Lei Heng nabbed him and brought him here. I pretended he was my nephew, and was able to save him. He told me: 'Governor Liang of Taming, the Northern Capital, has bought jewels and art objects worth a hundred thousand strings of cash to send to his father-in-law Premier Tsai in the Eastern Capital as birthday gifts. They will soon be passing this way. Since they were purchased with unclean money, there will be nothing wrong in taking them.' His proposal happens to coincide with a dream I just had. Last night I dreamed that the seven stars of the Big Dipper settled on the ridge of my roof. Another small star just above the handle turned into a streak of light. I thought to myself: To have stars shining right on your own house — that must be an auspicious sign. I intended to invite you over this morning, teacher, and ask you what I should do."

Wu Yung smiled. "I thought there was something odd about the sudden appearance of brother Liu, and was able to guess seven or eight-tenths of what was up. His proposal is excellent, but there's only one thing — with too many people involved, we can't succeed; with too few, we're bound to fail. Though you have many retainers here, not one of them is suitable. But can just the three of us accomplish our aim? Even though you, ward chief, and you, brother Liu, are remarkable people, the answer is no. What we need is seven or eight gallant men. More than that would be no use."

"Could that be the meaning of the number of stars in my dream?" asked Chao Kai.

"Brother's dream was no ordinary one," replied Wu Yung. "Can it be that north of here there are people who can help us?" Frowning he pondered for several moments. Then he understood. "There are, there are!" he exclaimed.

"If you know some courageous men you can trust, teacher," said Chao Kai, "invite them to join us and put this thing through."

Yang Chih Escorts a Convoy of Precious Goods;
Wu Yung Captures the Birthday Gifts by Guile

But enough of idle talk. Let's get back to Governor Liang in Taming, the Northern Capital. After buying birthday gifts valued at a hundred thousand strings of cash, he chose a date to start them on their way. The following day, as he held court in the rear hall, his wife, Madame Tsai, asked him:

"When will the birthday gifts go off, Your Excellency?"

"Tomorrow or the day after. I've bought everything I want. There's only one thing that's troubling me."

"What is it?"

"Last year I bought a hundred thousand strings of cash worth of jewels and art objects and sent them to the Eastern Capital, but because I didn't pick the right men they were seized by bandits on the road. To this day the robbers haven't been caught. At present I don't know of anyone really competent in my retinue. That is what's troubling me."

Madame Tsai pointed to a man standing at the foot of the steps. "Haven't you often said that this fellow is quite remark-

able? Why not entrust him with the mission? He can see it through!"

The man she indicated was Yang Chih, the Blue-faced Beast. Liang hesitated, then summoned Yang Chih into the hall.

"I had forgotten you," Liang said. "If you can safely deliver the birthday gifts for me, I'll have you raised in rank."

Yang Chih clasped his hands together respectfully. "Since that is what Excellency wishes, I must of course comply. How shall the convoy be composed, and when shall it set forth?"

"I'm ordering the prefectural government to supply ten large waggons, and will send ten soldiers of the city guard to escort them. Each waggon will carry a yellow banner reading: 'Convoy of Birthday Gifts to the Premier.' In addition, I will have one strong soldier follow each of the waggons. You can leave within the next three days."

"It's not that I'm unwilling, but I really can't do it. Please give the mission to some brave and skilful person."

"It's my desire to raise you in rank. Along with the birthday gift documents, I intend to include a letter to the premier, strongly recommending you for an official post. Why do you refuse to go?"

"Your servant has heard that the gifts were robbed last year, Your Excellency, and that to this day the bandits have not been caught. There are many brigands on the road these days. From here to the Eastern Capital there is no water route; you have to go entirely by land. Purple Gold Mountain, Two Dragons Mountain, Peach Blossom Mountain, Umbrella Mountain, Yellow Earth Ridge, White Sand Valley, Wild Clouds Ford, and Red Pine Forest – all must be crossed, and all are infested with bandits. No merchant dares travel through them alone. If the bandits know we're carrying a precious cargo, of course they'll want to seize it. We'll just be throwing our lives away! That is why I can't go."

"In that case I'll simply provide you with a larger military escort."

"Even if you gave me ten thousand men, it wouldn't solve anything, Your Excellency. Those craven oafs would run as soon as they heard the bandits coming."

"Do you mean to say that the birthday gifts can't be delivered?"

"If you'll grant your servant one request, I will undertake the mission."

"Since I'm willing to entrust you with it, why not? State your wish."

"As I see it, Your Excellency, we shouldn't use any waggons. Pack the gifts into containers to be carried on shoulder poles. I will dress like a merchant and disguise ten strong soldiers of the guard as porters. I'll need only one more person, also dressed as a merchant, to go as my assistant. We'll travel quietly day and night until we reach the Eastern Capital and deliver the goods. That way we'll be able to do it."

"It shall be as you wish. I'll write a letter to the premier strongly recommending you for an official appointment."

"My profoundest thanks, Excellency, for your gracious kindness."

That same day Yang Chih made up the loads and picked his soldiers. The following day he was again summoned to the rear hall. Governor Liang came out and asked: "Yang Chih, when will you be ready to leave?"

"We would like to start tomorrow morning, Your Excellency. I'm just waiting for the official documents."

"My wife has some gifts for her family. I want you to take them along too. I'm afraid you won't know your way around the premier's residence, so I'm sending with you Chief Steward Hsieh, husband of my wife's former wet nurse, and two couriers."

"I won't be able to go then, Excellency."

"Why not? The gifts are all packed in containers."

"I was made responsible for ten loads of gifts, and the soldiers were put in my charge. If I told them to march early, they'd march early. If I said late, then late it would be. They'd spend the night where I directed, and rest when I ordered it. Everything would be up to me. But now you also want to send the chief steward and two couriers. The steward is one of madame's men, the husband of a wet nurse in the premier's household. If he disagreed with me on the road how could I argue? Yet the blame would be mine if the mission failed."

"That's easy. I'll tell him and the couriers to do whatever you say."

"In that case, your servant is willing to accept the mission. May I be severely punished if I fail."

The governor was delighted. "I haven't decided to promote you in vain! You're a very sensible fellow!" Summoning Chief Steward Hsieh and the two couriers to the hall he gave them official orders: "Arms Instructor Yang Chih has accepted a mission to deliver birthday gifts — eleven loads of jewels and art objects — to the residence of the premier in the Eastern Capital. He is fully responsible. You three are to accompany him. During the journey he alone will decide whether to start early or late, where to spend the night, and when to rest. None of you is to cross him. You already know what madame wants done. Be cautious and prudent, leave soon and return quickly, don't let anything go wrong!"

The old chief steward promised to obey the governor's injunctions.

Before dawn the next morning the loads were lined up outside the main hall. The chief steward and the couriers brought another batch of valuables — making a total of eleven loads. Eleven strong soldiers of the guard were selected and disguised as porters. Yang Chih was wearing a broad-brimmed hat and a black silk tunic. His feet were shod in hemp sandals tied with laces of rope. In his waist was a dagger, and he carried a sword in his hand.

The old steward was also dressed as a merchant. The two couriers were disguised as lackeys. Each carried a sword and a rattan switch. Governor Liang handed over the official documents. After all had eaten their fill, they formally took their leave in front of the hall. Liang watched the soldiers raise the carrying poles to their shoulders and set forth. Together with Yang Chih, the old steward and the two couriers, a total of fifteen men left the governor's compound. Marching out of the Northern Capital's city gate, they proceeded down the highway in the direction of the Eastern Capital.

It was then the middle of the fifth lunar month.* Although the skies were clear, walking was difficult in the broiling sun. Determined to deliver the gifts in time for the premier's birthday on the fifteenth of the sixth lunar month, Yang Chih pushed the march along briskly. During the first week after the convoy left the Northern Capital, they set out every day before dawn to take advantage of the morning cool, and rested in the heat of noon. By the sixth or seventh day, dwellings were few and far between, travellers had thinned out, and the road began climbing into the mountains. Yang Chih now started the marches well after sunrise and didn't stop until late in the afternoon. The eleven guards were all carrying heavy loads and the weather was hot. Walking was a severe effort. Whenever they saw a grove they wanted to rest, but Yang Chih drove them on. If they halted, the least he did was curse them, and often he flogged them with his switch, forcing them to continue.

The two couriers, although they bore on their backs only some light luggage, gasped for breath and kept falling to the rear. Yang Chih berated them harshly: "How can you two be so ignorant? I'm responsible for this mission. Instead of helping me beat the porters, all you do is drag behind. This road is no place to dally!"

"It's not that we want to go slowly," said the couriers. "We just can't move any faster in this heat. A few days ago we always set out early when it was cool, but now we march only during the hottest hours of the day. Can't you tell the difference between fair conditions and foul?"

"Idiots! A few days ago we were in a good part of the country; now we're in a very ticklish place. We must march in broad daylight. Who dares to set out while it's still dark?"

The couriers said no more. But they thought to themselves: "That rogue swears at people whenever he likes!"

His sword in one hand, his switch in the other, Yang Chih urged on the convoy. The two couriers sat beneath a tree and

---

* June by the western calendar.

waited for the chief steward to catch up. "That murderous Yang Chih is only an arms instructor of His Excellency's guard," they complained to the old man. "What right has he to act so mighty?"

"The governor ordered us not to cross him. That's why I haven't said anything. These past few days I too have found him hard to bear. But we must be patient."

"His Excellency was only trying to make him feel good. You're the chief steward. Why don't you take over?"

"We must be patient with him," the old steward repeated.

That day they again marched until late afternoon. Then they stopped at an inn. Sweat was raining from the eleven porters. Groaning and sighing, they addressed the steward:

"Unfortunately we're soldiers of the guard, and have to go where we're ordered. For the past two days we've been carrying these heavy loads in the burning sun, instead of starting early when it's cool. For anything at all, we're given a taste of the switch. We're flesh and blood too. Why should we be treated so cruelly?"

"Don't complain," the steward urged them. "When we get to the Eastern Capital, I'll reward you personally."

"Of course we wouldn't have said anything, chief steward," they replied, "if we had someone like you looking after us."

Another night passed. The following morning everyone rose before daylight, hoping to march early while it was still cool. But Yang Chih jumped up and roared: "Where do you think you're going? Back to bed! I'll call you when it's time to leave!"

"We don't set out early," muttered the guards, "and in the heat of the day when we can't walk, he beats us!"

Swearing, Yang Chih yelled: "What do you clods understand!" He threatened them with his rattan switch. The soldiers had no choice but to swallow their complaints and return to bed.

After the sun had risen and everyone finished a leisurely breakfast, the convoy resumed its march. Yang Chih pushed on at a rapid pace, with no pauses for rest in the shade. The eleven guards grumbled constantly, and the two couriers made no end of peevish observations to the chief steward. Although the old man did not reply, in his heart he was very irritated with the leader of the expedition.

To make a long story short, after marching for fifteen days, there wasn't a man in the convoy who didn't hate Yang Chih. On the fourth day of the sixth month they again rose late and slowly cooked their own breakfast. Then they set out. Even before noon the sun was a fiery red ball on high. There wasn't a cloud in sight. It was really hot. Now they were travelling along winding mountain trails. Towering peaks looked down on them from all sides. After marching about twenty *li* the porters were longing to relax in the shade. Yang Chih lashed them with his switch.

"Move on," he shouted. "I'll teach you to rest before it's time!"

The guards looked up. There wasn't even half a cloud in the sky. The heat was simply unbearable. Yang Chih hurried the convoy along a path fringing the mountain. It was about noon then, and the stones were so hot they burned the porters' feet. Walking was extremely painful.

"A scorching day like this," groaned the guards. "You're killing us!"

"Hurry up!" Yang Chih urged. "First cross that ridge ahead, then we'll see."

The column of fifteen men hastened on until they mounted the earthen ridge. Then the porters lowered their carrying poles and threw themselves down beneath the pine trees.

"A fine place you've picked for cooling off!" Yang Chih ranted. "Get up, quick. We've got to push on."

"Even if you cut us into eight pieces, we can't move another step!" retorted the soldiers.

Yang Chih seized his switch and lashed them over the head and shoulders. But by the time he beat one to his feet another lay down again. He could do nothing with them. It was at this time that the old steward and the two couriers climbed panting to the top of the ridge and sat down beneath a pine, gasping for breath. When the old man saw Yang Chih belabouring the porters, he said:

"It's really much too hot to march, instructor. Forgive them."

"You don't understand, chief steward. This is Yellow Earth Ridge, a favourite haunt of bandits. Even in peaceful times they robbed here in broad daylight, to say nothing of what they do in times like these. Stopping here is very dangerous!"

"That's what you always say," countered the two couriers. "You just use those stories to scare people."

"Let the porters rest a bit," the steward urged. "We'll start again after noon, what do you say?"

"Impossible! Where's your judgment? For seven or eight *li* around the ridge there isn't a single house. Who dares rest in the shade in a place like this?" Yang Chih retorted.

"You go on with the porters first, then," said the steward. "I've got to sit a while."

Yang Chih picked up his rattan switch and roared at the soldiers: "Any man who doesn't march gets twenty blows of this!"

They all noisily protested. "Instructor," one of them cried, "while you walk empty-handed we're carrying well over a hundred catties apiece. You act as if we weren't even human! If the governor himself were in charge of this convoy, he'd at least let us say a word or two. You have no feeling at all! The only thing you know is to storm and rage!"

"What a sickening beast! A beating is all his kind understands!" Yang Chih rained blows on the man with his rattan switch.

"Stop, instructor!" shouted the steward. "Listen to me. In my days in the premier's residence I met thousands of officers, and every one of them treated me with deference. I don't mean to be rude, but it seems to me that an officer under sentence of death whom His Excellency has pitied and made an arms instructor of the guard—a post no bigger than a mustard seed—shouldn't be so pompous! Even if I were only a village elder, to say nothing of the governor's chief steward, you ought to heed my advice! Always beating the porters — what sort of conduct is that?"

"You're a city dweller, steward, born and raised in official residences. What do you know of the hardships of the road?"

"I've been as far as Szechuan, Kwangtung and Kwangsi, but I've never seen anyone who behaved like you!"

"You can't compare today with times of peace."

"Cut your tongue out! What's unpeaceful about today?"

Yang Chih was going to reply when he saw a shadowy figure poke his head out of a grove opposite and peer at them. "What did I tell you?" he shouted. "Isn't that a bad fellow over there?"

Flinging aside his switch, he seized his sword and charged into the grove, shouting: "Insolent villain! How dare you spy on our convoy?"

In the grove he found a line of seven wheel-barrows and six men, buff naked, resting in the shade. One of them, a fellow with a scarlet birthmark on the side of his temple, grabbed a sword when he saw Yang Chih advancing. The seven men cried in alarm: "*Aiya*!" and leaped to their feet.

"Who are you?" Yang Chih yelled.

"Who are you?" the seven countered.

"Aren't you robbers?"

"That's what we should be asking you! We're only poor merchants. We haven't any money to give you!"

"So you're poor merchants. And I suppose I'm rich!"

"Who are you, really?"

"Tell me first where you're from."

"We seven are from Haochow. We're bringing dates to sell in the Eastern Capital. At first we hesitated to pass this way because many people say that bandits often rob merchants on Yellow Earth Ridge. But then we said to ourselves: 'All we've got are some dates and nothing of any value.' So we decided to cross the ridge. Since the weather is so hot, we thought we'd rest in this grove till the cool of evening. When we heard you fellows coming up the rise we were afraid you might be bandits, so we sent this brother out for a look."

"So that's how it is – only ordinary merchants. I thought he was a robber when I saw him watching us, so I hurried in here to investigate."

"Please have some dates, sir," said the seven.

"No, thanks," replied Yang Chih. Sword in hand, he returned to the convoy.

"Since there are bandits around, we'd better leave!" said the chief steward, who was seated beneath a tree.

"I thought they were bandits, but they're only date merchants," Yang Chih explained.

"If it were like you said," the old steward remarked sarcastically, pointing his chin at the porters, "by now these fellows would all be dead!"

"No need to quarrel," said Yang Chih. "I only want everything to go well. You men can rest. We'll march on after it cools down a bit."

The guards smiled. Yang Chih stabbed the point of his sword into the ground, then he too sat down beneath a tree to rest and cool off.

In less time than it takes to eat half a bowl of rice, another man appeared in the distance. Carrying two buckets on the ends of a shoulder pole, he sang as he mounted the ridge:

Beneath a red sun that burns like fire,
Half scorched in the fields is the grain.
Poor peasant hearts with worry are scalded,
While the rich themselves idly fan!

Still singing, he walked to the edge of the pine grove, rested his buckets and sat down in the shade of a tree.

"What have you got in those buckets?" the soldiers asked him.

"White wine."

"Where are you going with it?"

"To the village, to sell."

"How much a bucket?"

"Five strings of cash — not a copper less."

The soldiers talked it over. "We're hot and thirsty. Why not buy some? It will ease the heat in our bodies." They all began chipping in.

"What are you fellows up to?" Yang Chih shouted, when he noticed what they were doing.

"We're going to buy a little wine."

Grasping the blade of his sword, Yang Chih flailed them with its hilt and swore. "What gall! How dare you buy wine without asking me?"

"Always raising a stinking fuss over nothing! It's our money! What is it to you if we buy wine? He beats us for that, too!"

"What do you stupid bastards know anyhow? You see wine and all you can think of is guzzling! But not a thought do you give to all the tricks that are pulled on the road! Do you know how many good men have been toppled by drugs?"

The wine vendor looked at Yang Chih and laughed coldly. "You don't know much yourself, master merchant! I wasn't going to sell you any in the first place. What a dirty thing to say about a man's wine!"

As they were quarrelling, the date merchants emerged from the grove, swords in hand. "What's the trouble?" they asked.

"I was carrying this wine across the ridge to sell in the village and stopped to cool off when these fellows asked if they could buy some," the vendor said. "I didn't let them have any. Then this merchant claimed my wine was drugged. Is he trying to be funny, or what?"

"*Pei*!" snorted the seven. "We thought robbers had come, at least! So that's what all the row was about. Suppose he did say it – so what? We were just thinking of having some wine. If they're suspicious, sell a bucket to us. We'll drink it."

"No, no! Nothing doing!" said the vendor.

"We didn't say anything against you, you stupid clod," cried the seven. "We'll give you the same price you'd get in the village. If you sell to us, what's the difference? You'll be doing a good deed, like handing out tea on a hot day, and quenching our thirst at the same time."

"I don't mind selling you a bucket, but they said my wine is bad. Besides, I don't have any dipper."

"You take things too seriously! What do you care what they said? We have our own dippers."

Two of the date merchants brought out two coconut ladles from one of the wheel-barrows, while a third scooped up a big handful of dates. Then the seven gathered around the bucket and removed its cover. Ladling out the wine in turn, they drank, while munching the dates. Before long the bucket was empty.

"We haven't asked you the price yet," said the seven.

"I never bargain," the vendor asserted. "Exactly five strings of cash per bucket – ten strings for the load."

"Five strings you say, then five strings it shall be. But give us one free scoop out of the other bucket."

"Can't be done. My prices are fixed!"

While one of the date merchants paid him the money, another opened the cover of the second bucket, ladled up some wine and started to drink it. The vendor hurried towards him, but the man walked quickly into the pine grove with the half consumed dipper of wine. As the vendor hastened after him, another merchant emerged from the grove with another ladle. He dipped this into the bucket and raised to his lips. The vendor rushed over, seized the ladle, and dumped its contents back into the bucket. Replacing the cover, he flung the ladle to the ground.

"You look like a proper man – why don't you act like one?" he fumed. "Is that any way to behave?"

When the soldiers saw this, their throats felt even drier. All were longing for a drink. "Put in a word for us, old grandpa," one of them begged the chief steward. "Those date merchants drank a bucket of his wine. Why shouldn't we buy the other and wet our throats? We're hot and thirsty, and we haven't any other way. There's no place to get water on this ridge. Do us a favour, old grandpa!"

The old steward heard them out. He felt like having a drink himself. So he conferred with Yang Chih.

"Those date merchants have already finished a bucket of that vendor's wine. Only one bucket is left. Why not let them buy some wine and ward off heat stroke? There really isn't any place on this ridge to get water."

Yang Chih thought to himself: "I watched those birds finish off his first bucket, and drink half a ladleful from the second. The wine must be all right. I've been beating our porters for hours. Maybe I ought to let them buy a few drinks."

Aloud, he said: "Since the chief steward suggests it, you rogues can have some wine. Then we'll march on."

The soldiers chipped in and raised the price of a bucket. But the vendor refused them. "I'm not selling, I'm not selling!" he said angrily. "This wine is drugged!"

"Don't be like that, brother," the soldiers said with placating smiles. "Why rub it in?"

"I'm not selling," said the vendor, "so don't hang around!"

The date merchants intervened. "Stupid oaf!" they berated him. "What if that fellow said the wrong thing? You're much too serious. You've even tried to take it out on us. Anyhow, it has nothing to do with these porters. Sell them some wine and be done with it."

"And give him a chance to cast suspicion on me for no reason at all?" the vendor demanded.

The date merchants pushed him aside and handed the bucket to the soldiers, who removed the cover. Having no ladles, they apologetically asked the merchants if they could borrow theirs.

"Have some dates, also, to go with your wine," said the merchants.

"You're very kind!"

"No need to be polite. We're all travellers together. What do a hundred or so dates matter?"

The soldiers thanked them. The first two ladles of wine they presented to Yang Chih and the chief steward. Yang Chih refused, but the old man drank his. The next two ladlefuls were consumed by the two couriers. Then the soldiers swarmed around the bucket and imbibed heartily.

Yang Chih wavered. The soldiers showed no ill effects. Besides, the weather was hot and his throat was parched. Scooping up half a ladle of wine, he drank it while munching on a few dates.

"That date merchant drank a ladleful out of this bucket, so you had less wine," the vendor said to the soldiers. "You can pay me half a string of cash less."

The soldiers gave him his money. The vendor took it, then, carrying his shoulder pole and empty buckets, he swung off down the ridge, again singing a folk song.

Standing on the edge of the pine grove, the seven date merchants pointed at the fifteen men of the convoy and said: "Down you go! Down you go!" The fifteen, weak in the knees and heavy in the head, stared at each other as, one by one, they sank to the ground. Then the seven merchants pushed the seven wheel-barrows out of the grove and dumped the dates. Placing the eleven loads of jewels and art objects into the barrows, they covered them over. "Sorry to trouble you!" they called, and trundled off down the ridge.

Yang Chih, too weak to move, could only groan inwardly. The fifteen couldn't get up. They had only been able to goggle helplessly while the seven had loaded the barrows with the precious cargo. They were paralysed, bereft of speech.

Now I ask you — who were those seven men? None other than Chao Kai, Wu Yung, Kungsun Sheng, Liu Tang and the three Yuan brothers. And the wine vendor was Pai Sheng, nicknamed "Rat Who Steals in Broad Daylight." And how was the wine drugged? When the buckets were carried up the ridge, they contained pure wine. After the seven finished the first bucket, Liu Tang removed the cover from the second and deliberately drank half a ladleful so as to dull the others' suspicions. Next, inside the grove, Wu Yung poured the drug into the other ladle. Then he came out and spilled it into the wine while taking a "free scoop." As he pretended to drink, Pai Sheng grabbed the ladle and dumped the wine back in the bucket.

That was the ruse. Planned entirely by Wu Yung, it can be called "Capturing the Birthday Gifts by Guile."

Yang Chih had not drunk much, and he recovered quickly. Crawling to his feet, he could hardly stand. He looked at the other fourteen. Saliva was running from the corners of their mouths. None of them could move.

"You've made me lose the birthday gifts," he muttered in angry despair. "How can I even face Governor Liang again? These convoy documents are worthless now!" He tore them up. "I've become a man without a home or country. Where can I go? Better that I should die right here on this ridge!" Clutching his tunic, he staggered to the edge of the ridge and prepared to jump.

Truly: *Rains in the third month wash the fallen blossoms away, the last of willow tendrils the autumn frosts destroy.*

SQUIRE CH'AI CHIN DETAINS A GUEST; WU SUNG KILLS A TIGER

WE have already related how Sung Chiang, in order to avoid drinking more wine, went outside to the toilet and while on the veranda he upset the charcoal brazier, and burnt a man, and how this resulted in Sung Chiang's name being disclosed to the man. When the man heard Sung Chiang's name how could he get up after kotowing? He said, "I failed to recognize your eminence and I hope that you will forgive me for that blunder."

Sung Chiang raised him up and asked who he was.

"This man," said Ch'ai Chin, "is Wu Sung of Ching Ho Hsien, and he is a second son. He has lived here for a year."

"I have often heard of Wu Erh-lang, but I did not expect to meet him here to-day. What a good luck!" said Sung Chiang.

"It is very unusual for heroes to meet in this way. I request you both to come and have some wine with me," said Ch'ai Chin.

Sung Chiang was much pleased at this and taking Wu Sung by the hand conducted him to the hall where he summoned Sung Ching and introduced him to Wu Sung. Ch'ai Chin then invited Wu Sung to be seated, and Sung Chiang strongly urged him to take the premier position at the table. But Wu Sung was unwilling to take the place of honor, and after politely declining for a long time he at last took his seat in the third position. Ch'ai Chin ordered the servants to spread a feast with wine, and when ready he strongly pressed his guests to partake the same.

Sung Chiang was exceedingly pleased with the manner and bearing of Wu Sung, and at last he asked him why he was staying there.

"While I was at Ching Ho Hsien I got drunk and had a fight with some official. I struck him with my fist while I was in a very hot temper, and knocked him nearly insensible. I thought I had killed him, so in order to avoid being arrested I ran away to this place for refuge where I have stayed for more than a year. Afterwards I heard that the man I had struck had not died—he was still alive. I would have liked to return home and found my elder brother, but I felt ill and was unable to go. When you overturned the charcoal brazier on the veranda I was very much alarmed, and had a heavy cold perspiration, but I think that had cured my sickness."

Sung Chiang was much pleased upon hearing this. The feast lasted till nearly midnight. Then Sung Chiang took Wu Sung to a very comfortable room on the west side where they both slept that night. The next day Ch'ai Chin arranged another feast at which a sheep and a pig were served.

After a few days Sung Chiang gave Wu Sung some money to buy clothing. When Ch'ai Chin heard of this he wondered how he could let it be done. So he took some rolls of silk and satin, and told his own family tailor to make three suits for them. But Ch'ai Chin had not made such a present before so why did he do it now?

The reason was that when Wu Sung first came there for refuge he had been treated as a guest, but he was often drunk. Whenever the servants did not treat him well he would become angry and beat them, and therefore there was not a single servant who had a good word for him. They all hated him, and often complained to Ch'ai Chin about his conduct. But Ch'ai Chin would not speak to him about this and only became more distant in his manner towards his guest. When Sung Chiang came he sought out Wu Sung, and they used to drink wine in each other's company every day. Soon Wu Sung's bad temper had vanished. After about ten days of this mutual friendship Wu Sung thought of returning to Ching Ho Hsien to visit his elder brother. He was pressed not to go by Ch'ai Chin and Sung Chiang, but after a little time he spoke to them saying, "I have not heard from my elder brother for a long time so I must go and see him."

"As you want to go," said Sung Chiang, "we do not wish to upset you by detaining you. But I hope that we shall meet again at some future date."

Wu Sung expressed his thanks, and Ch'ai Chin gave him

some gold and silver. Wu Sung again expressed his thanks, and regretted that he had given them so much trouble. After a parting cup Wu Sung made up his bundle, and slung it on his back. He wore a red-silk-quilted coat similar to those worn by priests, and had a white felt cap which was made in Fanyang style. He carried a cudgel in his hand.

Just as he was about to depart Sung Chiang asked him to wait a bit, and then went into his own room, and taking some silver met Wu Sung at the gate saying, "I will accompany you for a short distance." Sung Ching also came with his brother Sung Chiang and as the three were taking leave of Ch'ai Chin, Sung Chiang said, "Sir, I shall be gone only for a short distance."

When the three had traveled about a couple of miles Wu Sung urged the brothers to return as Ch'ai Chin would undoubtedly be getting anxious.

"What objection can there be for us to go a few steps further?" said Sung Chiang.

So they went on for about a mile more chatting on the way, and then Wu Sung took Sung Chiang by the hand and said, "You must not come any further. People often say, 'Even if you accompany a guest three hundred miles you must at last come to the parting place.'"

"I will go a few steps further," said Sung Chiang. "Just over there, there is a small inn where we can drink a few cups of wine before parting."

When they reached the inn Sung Chiang took the seat of honor, and Wu Sung took the lower position after placing his cudgel by his chair. Sung Ching sat at the side of the table. They told the waiter to bring fruit and vegetables which were duly supplied. After they had been drinking wine for some time they noticed the red hues of sunset, and Wu Sung said, "It is getting late and we had better separate and I will give you four salutations as my adopted elder brother." Sung Chiang was much pleased. Wu Sung kotowed four times, and Sung Chiang then told his brother Sung Ching to take ten ounces of silver and presented it to Wu Sung. But Wu Sung declined to accept it, and asked them to reserve it for they themselves were guests at another's home.

"You must not be so anxious about us, younger brother," said Sung Chiang. "If you decline it I cannot recognize you as my younger brother."

So Wu Sung took the money. He then shouldered his bundle, and taking his cudgel the three walked hand in hand to the door where they separated with tears in the eyes. The brothers stood at the door of the inn until Wu Sung could no longer be seen, and then they departed for home. When they had gone less than two miles they met Ch'ai Chin riding a horse, and leading two spare ones to welcome them home. They were highly delighted at this, and mounted. They soon reached the village. Upon dismounting they all went into a hall at the back where they drank wine, and after this the two brothers stayed with Ch'ai Chin.

When Wu Sung left the brothers he traveled some distance, and then rested for the night at an inn. The next morning after an early breakfast he started on the road again. As he walked he ruminated that all men had said that the Welcome Rain, Sung Chiang, was truly a fine man, and he had certainly been well treated by him. After a few days he was approaching Yang Ku Hsien about noon when he felt very hungry and thirsty.

Just then he happened to see an inn with a signboard over the door with five characters, meaning, "If you drink three cups of our wine you will be unable to cross the mountain ridge."

Wu Sung entered the inn, took his seat, placed his cudgel by his side, and called the proprietor to bring some wine. The proprietor put before him three cups, a tray with some cooked vegetables, and a pair of chopsticks. The proprietor then slowly fill a cup with wine. Wu Sung picked up the cup and drank the wine off saying, "This wine is very strong. I wish to have some food, to take with more wine."

"I have some roast beef," said the proprietor.

"That is fine. Bring me about four pounds of beef."

The proprietor soon brought in a plate of beef and setting it before Wu Sung, he again poured out a cup of wine. Wu Sung drank the wine and again praised it. The proprietor filled another cup, and then left him.

As the proprietor had not returned Wu Sung banged the

table and called out, "Proprietor, why do you not serve more wine?"

"If you want more beef I can let you have some," said the man.

"I want wine as well as beef."

"I can give you beef, but no more wine," said the man.

"That is strange!" said Wu Sung. "Why don't you give me wine while I can pay for it?"

"Did you not see the signboard over the door of this inn?" asked the man.

"What is the idea of such a signboard?" asked Wu Sung.

"Although our wine is made here yet it has a very delicate flavor," said the man. "Whenever a guest arrives and drinks three cups of this wine he always gets drunk so that he cannot go over the mountain ridge, and that is why I put up that signboard. When guests stop here they never ask for more than three cups of wine."

"That is the case," said Wu Sung laughingly. "But how is it that I am not drunk after three cups?"

"Our wine is called 'T'ou Ping Hsiang' (the aroma penetrates the bottle), and also has another name, which means 'upon leaving the door you will fall down.' While drinking, it has a fine flavor, but in a short time afterwards you will fall down."

"Don't talk nonsense," said Wu Sung. "I won't cheat you; I'll pay you, so bring me three more cups of wine."

The proprietor saw that he was not in the least affected by the wine so he filled three more cups.

After drinking Wu Sung said, "It is really very fine. I want you to keep on pouring out the wine, and I will pay you for each cup I drink."

"Sir, please give up the idea of drinking any more or you will undoubtedly be drunk, and there is no medicine to prevent it."

"You need not speak such rubbish," said Wu Sung. "If you put some drug in the wine I should soon detect it."

The innkeeper could find no answer to this so he poured out three more cups of wine.

Wu Sung ordered a further four pounds of beef. The innkeeper brought in the cold beef and again poured out three cups of wine. Wu Sung drank the wine, but still wanted more. So he took out his silver and showing it to the innkeeper asked, "Look at this. Is it enough for your wine and beef?"

"More than enough!" said the innkeeper. "Let me have it and I will give you the balance."

"I do not want any change," said Wu Sung. "You can pay me the balance in wine."

"Sir," said the innkeeper, "you have had a lot of wine, but I still have five or six cups full left. But I am afraid that you will not be able to drink so much."

"As you have about five cups of wine more you can let me have the whole lot," said Wu Sung.

"You are a very big man," said the innkeeper, "and how am I going to lift you up when you fall down dead drunk?"

"I should not be a man, should I want you to help me up," said Wu Sung.

But the innkeeper was unwilling to pour out any more wine, so Wu Sung spoke in an angry tone, "Have I not paid you for the wine! Do not provoke me to anger or I shall smash the whole room into atoms, and turn your inn upside down."

The innkeeper saw that Wu Sung was drunk so he decided not to oppose him and poured out all the six cups of wine. Altogether Wu Sung drank eighteen cups of wine, and then picking up his cudgel he got up and said, "I am not drunk yet!" He walked to the door laughing, and proceeded on his way.

The innkeeper however called after him, "Sir, where are you going?"

"Why do you call me?" replied Wu Sung. "Have I not paid you for the wine?"

"I have a good intention for you," said the innkeeper. "I want you to come to my home and look at a copy of an official proclamation."

"What is the proclamation about?" asked Wu Sung.

"Just now there is, on Ching Yang Ridge, a large animal with a white forehead and protruding eyes. It comes out in the evening, and has already killed about thirty men, and injured many others. The magistrate has enjoined upon the hunters to catch the animal by a certain time. At all crossroads there is a notice warning travelers of the danger, and ordering them to band themselves together when crossing the ridge. Travelers must cross the ridge only between the hours of 9 a. m. and 3 p. m. and not at any other time. So that, as you are by yourself you must wait and join with some other travelers before you can cross the ridge. It is now well past three o'clock and yet I see you walking off without asking anyone to go with you, and evidently you are running the risk of your life. It will be better if you stay here for the night, and go over the ridge to-morrow in the company of about thirty men."

"I am a Ching Ho Hsien man," laughed Wu Sung, "and although I have been across the Ching Yang Ridge about twenty times I have never seen or heard of a big animal there. So you need not talk like this just to frighten me. And even if there is a beast I am not afraid of it."

"I only wanted to save your life," said the innkeeper "If you do not believe what I say then come inside and read the official proclamation."

"You need not say anything further," said Wu Sung. "Even if there is a tiger I shall not be afraid. I suppose if I pass the night at your inn you may try to get my money during the night, and perhaps kill me. That is why you now make up this story to frighten me and keep me here."

"Look here!" said the innkeeper. "I am taking good care of you, yet you think I have bad intention. If you do not believe what I say then go your own way." While saying this he shook his head with regret, and entered his inn.

Wu Sung picked up his cudgel and started off for the Ching Yang Ridge. After walking about two miles he reached the foot of the ridge, and there he saw a large tree which had had its bark taken away, and on the white timber were two columns of characters written. It was to the same effect as the official proclamation.

On reading it Wu Sung laughed and said, "This is the artful intimidation of that innkeeper who wants to frighten travelers so that they will stay at his inn. But I am not afraid." Dragging his cudgel along the ground he proceeded on his way. It was about four o'clock, and the sun was slowly sinking behind the ridge, setting the sky in a red evening glow. The large quantities of wine he had drunk had driven all fear away so he proceeded on his way. He had only gone a little distance when he saw a ruined temple, and on the door was another notice so he went forward and read it. It warned travelers of the danger of crossing the ridge.

So Wu Sung at last realized that there was a tiger to be faced, and his first thought was to return to the inn. But he saw in that case the innkeeper would only laugh at him, and regard him as a coward—so that would not do. But after a second thought, he said to himself, "Why be afraid? Why not face the danger?" He went on, but soon vomited the wine he had taken. He then took his cap, and pushed it on his back suspended by the tapes. He put his cudgel under his arm, and slowly ascended the ridge. Turning his head he saw that the sun had now sunk to the west. It was now the tenth moon so that the days were short, the nights long, and the sunset was soon followed by darkness.

He soliloquized, "Where is that tiger that men are so afraid of that they dare not cross the ridge?" He went a little further, and now felt the effect of the wine. So taking the cudgel in one hand he unloosened his coat with the other hand. Staggering along he entered the forest. He came across a large block of smooth green stone against which he put his cudgel. He then reclined on the stone with the intention of sleeping there. Just then a strong wind sprang up, and he heard a sound among the trees, and at the same moment a large tiger sprang out. With an exclamation he rolled off the stone, seized his cudgel, and slipped to one side of the stone. The tiger was both hungry and thirsty, and crouched on the ground ready for a spring. As the tiger sprang forward Wu Sung was startled, and was covered with a cold sweat, but slipping to one side he escaped. The tiger immediately turned round, and roared like thunder, so that the ridge almost quaked.

The tiger's tail was erect and stiff as a poker, and was lashed from side to side in rage. Wu Sung did not keep still, but kept moving about irregularly. In fact the tiger had only three methods of killing men, a crouch, a leap, and a blow with its tail. If these three failed, the tiger at once lost all courage or spirit. In such cases it always turned round, and gave a loud roar. When Wu Sung saw it turning round seized his cudgel with both hands, and using the utmost of his strength he whirled it aloft, and brought it down with a crash. There was a great noise followed by a fall of leaves and twigs from the dense undergrowth. Wu Sung saw that he had missed the tiger, and simply in his haste had hit the undergrowth. As his long cudgel was broken in half, he threw a part away. The tiger roared again, crouched, and again leapt at Wu Sung. Wu Sung again swiftly stepped to one side. The tiger whirled round and came just in front of Wu Sung and planted its fore paws on the ground. Wu Sung threw the remaining half of the cudgel away, and seized the tiger's forehead skin with both hands, and pressed the tiger down on the ground. The tiger struggled to get up, but Wu Sung exerted all his strength, and would not let it go the least bit. He kicked it in the eyes. This made the tiger roar, and scoop out holes in the yellow soil with its front paws. Wu Sung now pressed the tiger's snout into the hole in the ground, and it had to endure this disgrace as it was losing its strength. Wu Sung now grasped the loose skin on the tiger's head in his left hand, and taking his right fist hit the tiger severely. After about seventy blows blood streamed out of the tiger's eyes, mouth, nose, and ears, and the beast lay panting for breath. Wu Sung left it for a moment, and went to get a part of his cudgel. As he was afraid that the tiger was not yet dead he dealt the tiger some blows for some time until he saw evidently that it was no longer alive. He thereupon threw away his cudgel and wondered whether he should drag the tiger down the mountain. The body lay in a pool of blood, and using both hands he tried to move it, but he found that it was too heavy. He had used up all his strength so that he now felt weak in hand and foot. So he sat down on the green smooth stone for a short rest, and meditated that the night was quite dark now, and what could he do if another tiger were to attack him. So he decided to leave the ridge and return the following day for the tiger's body. He looked around and found his felt cap, and then started down the mountain.

He had not gone far when he saw two tigers emerging from the dry grass. "Ai Ya!" he said. "That's all gone now." But he noticed that the two tigers now stood up on their hind legs, and looking closely he saw that they were two men who had fastened tiger skins very closely on their bodies, and carried in their hands five-pronged forks.

They were surprised at seeing Wu Sung, and said, "You. . . . you . . . you. . . , you must have eaten the heart of a wolf, the gall bladder of a leopard, and the legs of a lion so that your whole body becomes a mass of courage. How dare you to cross the ridge during the night without a single weapon in your hand. You. . . . you. . . . you. . . . are you a man or a devil?"

"But who are you?" asked Wu Sung.

"We are native hunters," replied the men.

"And what are you doing on this mountain?" asked Wu Sung.

The men were surprised at such a question and asked, "Do you mean to say that you do not know? On this mountain there is a dangerous tiger which attacks men at night, and has already injured eight hunters, and numerous travelers have been killed. The district magistrate has ordered us, and also the village headman, to come here to catch the tiger. But its strength is so great that it is difficult to come near it. Who dare face it? The magistrate has beaten us repeatedly for not catching the tiger, but it makes no difference. To-night we have come here, accompanied by ten men from the villages, and we are all over the mountain, armed with poisoned arrows, waiting for the tiger. Just here we lay in ambush when we saw you coming from the mountain as bold as brass, and it gave us quite a start. Who are you? Have you seen the tiger?"

"I am a Ching Ho Hsien man, and my name is Wu Sung. When I got up the mountain I met the tiger, and killed it with my fist and foot."

"It is impossible," said the hunters aghastly.

"You do not believe," said Wu Sung. "But do you see the bloodstains on my clothes?"

"But how did you kill it?"

Wu Sung then gave them all the details of his fighting with the tiger.

The hunters were both amazed and amused, and then summoned the ten villagers. The villagers soon arrived and armed with pronged forks, crossbows, swords, and spears.

"How is it that these men did not stay with you here?" asked Wu Sung.

The hunters said, "The animal was very fierce, so how could they dare to come on the mountain?"

When the villagers had all assembled in front of them, the hunters asked Wu Sung to recite to them how he had killed the tiger. He did so, but they did not believe what he said.

"Well," said Wu Sung, "if you do not believe then I will go, and show you the dead animal."

The villagers had flint and steel, and they then used them to strike lights and ignite torches. They went with Wu Sung, and soon came to the top of the ridge where they were shown the dead tiger. They were highly delighted, and immediately sent men to report the matter to the headman of the district. The men who were left behind, tied up the carcass, and carried it on their shoulders down the mountain. At the foot of the mountain there were already about eighty men waiting for them, and they made an uproar when they saw the dead tiger. They carried the tiger in front and put Wu Sung in a sedan chair. The whole party then started off to the nearest village reporting to the headman there.

Upon arriving there, there were two headmen waiting outside the village to welcome them. The party was conducted to the main room of a cottage where the other hunters of the village and about thirty other men all came to have an interview with Wu Sung. He then told them in detail his recent adventure.

They all declared that he was a very brave hero, and brought him some food and wine. But Wu Sung was very tired, and wanted to rest. So the servants were told to prepare a bedroom for him where he slept that night.

The next morning a messenger was dispatched to report the matter to the district magistrate and a litter was prepared to carry the tiger's body to the town.

When Wu Sung got up and had washed his face, he found in front of the building a large number of men bringing a sheep and a jar of wine which they offered to him as their gifts. They said, "We do not know exactly how many people that beast has killed, or how many bamboo blows our hunters have received, but now you have killed the tiger, and our trouble has come an end. We are very happy indeed. Moreover, the travelers can go without danger, and all this is due to your bounteous action."

"It was not due to my skill but was owing to your fortune," replied Wu Sung.

The people all saluted him. After an exhilarating feast which lasted all the morning they placed the tiger's body on the litter which was ready. They made garland of silk and red flowers for Wu Sung. They were about to start off from the village. A deputy of the district magistrate had already arrived to conduct Wu Sung to the court. Four men were sent with a cool sedan chair to convey Wu Sung to the court. The litter with the tiger's carcass was in front of the procession and it was also decorated with red flowers and pieces of silk. When the people of the town heard of the great hero who had killed a tiger on the mountain they all crowded to see him, and made such a noise that it could be heard all over the district. Wu Sung in his chair saw all the streets were blocked with noisy crowds which were eager to have a look at the tiger. Upon reaching the yamen gate, he saw the district magistrate waiting in the hall. The litter and the sedan chair were carried to the court, and laid in the corridor in front of the door.

The magistrate noticed the manner of Wu Sung, and also the size of the tiger. He thought that Wu Sung was the only person who could kill such a tiger. He summoned Wu Sung to come forward. Wu Sung approached and called out "ngo." The magistrate invited him inside where Wu Sung recited his adventure. There was a large crowd of men both inside and outside the hall. They all listened to Wu Sung and were greatly astonished. The magistrate offered several cups of wine to Wu Sung, and also a gift of one thousand strings of cash which had been subscribed by the wealthy families of the district.

"I am grateful to you for this blessing, sir," said Wu Sung. "I was fortunate in killing the tiger, and as it was not due to my own abilities, how dare I accept such generous presents? I have heard that these hunters have been beaten with the bamboo, so why not compensate them with these strings of cash?"

"As you, the hero, suggest this, it can be done as you

wish," said the magistrate.

So Wu Sung took the strings of cash, and distributed them among the hunters.

When the magistrate saw the noble, virtuous,and benevolent character of Wu Sung he wished to recommend him for an official post. So he said to him, "You are a Ching Ho Hsien man, and as that place is quite close here I offer you the position of lieutenant in this yamen. What do you say about that?"

Wu Sung knelt down and said, "As you wish to reward me in this way I shall be obliged to you for my life."

The magistrate instructed his secretary to make out the necessary papers, and Wu Sung received his commission in the army as a lieutenant.

The rich families saluted him, and offered their congratulations, and during the following five days they continually entertained him with wine.

Wu Sung meditated that, at first, he had the idea to find his elder brother, but it was detained by being made a lieutenant at this place. The magistrate liked him, and his fame was widespread in every village.

One day when he was strolling outside the yamen he heard a voice behind him calling, "Lieutenant Wu! As you are an official now, can you not assist me?"

"Ai Ya!" exclaimed Wu Sung when he turned round. "What are you doing here?"

If these heroes had not met,
  Many men would not have died;
Swords would not have chopped off heads,
  Nor blood have flown like water.

THE FALSE LI K'WEI COMMITS HIGHWAY ROBBERY; THE BLACK WHIRLWIND KILLS FOUR TIGERS ON I LING

LI K'WEI had asked for the three conditions, and Sung Chiang replied, "When you go to I Shui Hsien, in I Chou, Shantung province to bring your mother here you must not drink wine on the way. That is the first condition. Secondly, you must go by yourself, because you have a hasty disposition and I am afraid that nobody wants to go with you. Thirdly, you must not take those axes with you, and on the way you must be discreet, and quickly get back here."

"I can easily comply with those conditions," said Li K'wei. "You need not worry. I should like to leave to-day." On that day he got his baggage ready, armed himself with two swords. He took one large ingot, and about five small pieces of silver. He drank a few cups of wine, took leave of his companions, and then went down the hill and across the lake.

After his departure the leaders were assembled in the main hall when Sung Chiang spoke, "I am afraid that our younger brother Li K'wei will get into trouble. I do not know whether there is any man here from his village. If so he might follow him, and report to us what happens on the way."

"Chu Kwei comes from the same village as Li K'wei," said Tu Chien.

"I had forgotten that," said Sung Chiang. "Of course they recognized each other as such at the White Dragon Temple near Chiang Chou." He immediately sent a man to summon Chu Kwei, and soon the latter arrived from his inn.

"Our brother, Li K'wei, has just gone to I Shui Hsien to bring his mother here. No man was sent to accompany him on account of his bad temper, when drunk. I understand that you are from his native district, and therefore I should be glad if you would follow him, and watch what might happen to him."

"I am a I Shui Hsien man," said Chu Kwei. "I have a younger brother who keeps a wine shop in that town just outside the West Gate. This man Li K'wei lived near a village called Po Chang in that district. He has an elder brother named Li Ta who is in regular employment. Li K'wei is a fierce and stupid man. Some time ago he committed murder at his village, and had to leave home, and dared not return. I have no objection to follow him, and look after him, but who will look after my inn while I am away? I have not been home for a long time, and should very much like to meet my brother again."

"You need not worry about your inn as I will send Hou Chien and Shih Yung to look after it during your absence," said Sung Chiang.

This was all arranged, and Chu Kwei started off on his way to I Shui Hsien.

Li K'wei traveled by himself, and duly reached his destination. He had stuck to the conditions laid down by Sung Chiang, and had not taken any wine on the way. At the West Gate he saw a big crowd of men reading a proclamation posted on the wall. He entered the crowd and listened to a man who was reading the proclamation for the information of the illiterate crowd. It read as follows: "(1) There is a thief called Sung Chiang of Yun Cheng Hsien; (2) Also a jailer named Tai Tsung, from the prison at Chiang Chou; (3) Also another thief named Li K'wei, of I Shui Hsien." As soon as he heard his own name Li K'wei got excited, and did not know what to do when a man embraced him saying, "Elder brother Chang, what are you doing here?" Upon looking at the man he recognized him as Chu Kwei, the Speedy Courier, and asked, "And what are you doing here?"

"Come with me and we will discuss matters," said Chu Kwei. They went together outside the town, and stopped at an inn in a small hamlet, where they entered a small room at the back of the premises.

Chu Kwei pointed at Li K'wei, "What a nerve you have! That proclamation was offering a reward of ten thousand strings of cash for the arrest of Sung Chiang; five thousand strings for Tai Tsung, and three thousand strings of cash for your arrest. Why did you stop there looking at such a notice? Should any man recognize you you would be arrested at once. Sung Chiang was afraid that you would get into trouble, and sent me here to watch over you. I left the mountain a day after your departure, and arrived here a day before you. What has delayed you?"

"It is due to Sung Chiang ordering me not to drink wine," said Li K'wei. "I walked slowly because of that. Do you know anyone at this inn? Where is your home in this place?"

"This inn belongs to my younger brother, Chu Fu, and I used to live here. I was once a merchant, but lost all my capital, and so went to Liang Shan Po. I have not been here since that time." He called for his brother, and introduced Li K'wei to him. Chu Fu then brought in some wine and invited them to partake of same.

"Our elder brother gave me an order not to drink wine," said Li K'wei. "But as I am no longer on the road and have reached my destination, I may drink two cups of wine now."

Chu Kwei raised no objection to this, and they stayed eating and drinking there until nearly 2 a.m. It was a bright moonlight night and Li K'wei wished to go, but Chu Kwei said, "You had better avoid the byroad, but turn round to the east when you come to a clump of trees and that will bring you to your home at Po Chang Village. You must bring your mother here, without delay, and we will set off at once for Liang Shan Po."

"I will go along the byroads, and will lose no time," replied Li K'wei.

"By that unfrequented road there are tigers and also bandits," said Chu Kwei.

"What am I afraid of?" asked Li K'wei. He then armed himself with his two swords, and left the two brothers. When he had gone about three miles it was getting daylight, he saw a hare leap out of the grass at the side of the path, and race off along the road. He pursued his way, and in about two miles came to the clump of trees, with leaves of red autumn tints. As he turned round the trees he met a big man who shouted, "You will be aware that if you pay us money we will not interfere with your baggage."

The man wore a coat of rough cloth and had a red silk turban. His face was sallow, and he held an ax in each hand.

Li K'wei shouted, "Who are you that dare commit highway robbery here?"

"If I told you my name you would be frightened. I am called the Black Whirlwind. If you pay our toll we will spare your life."

Li K'wei laughed loudly, "How dare you use my own name in this way? Who are you, and where do you come from, you barefaced rascal?" He took his sword and advanced towards the man.

The man saw that he had a very strong opponent and tried to retreat, but Li K'wei struck him with his sword so that he fell to the ground. Li K'wei put his foot on the man's breast and asked, "Do you know me now?"

The man on the ground said, "Please forgive me, sir."

"I am Li K'wei, the Black Whirlwind. Why do you use my name in this way?"

The man replied, "My name is Li, but I am not the Black Whirlwind. You have a great name, and if I use it people are afraid of me. It was because I found out the power of your name that I became a highwayman. I only stop single individuals, and as soon as they hear your name they drop their baggage and run away. I do not kill people, and yet I make a little profit. My name is Li, the Devil, and I live at the village a little up the road."

Li K'wei said, "You are a rowdy fellow. You seize traveler's baggage, and also carry axes in both hands like me, so that you injure my reputation. You can taste one of my axes," so saying he seized an ax out of the man's hand.

Li, the Devil, called out, "Sir, if you kill me you will kill two persons."

"How do you make that out?" asked Li K'wei, staying the blow.

"At home I support my mother who is ninety years of age, and this is my only means of helping her in her old age," said Li, the Devil. "I never injure people, but only make them afraid. If you kill me, my old mother will die of starvation."

This man (Li K'wei) who never twinkled his eyes in chopping off people's heads, paused and thought when he heard this. "Here am I trying to succour my old mother, and yet killing a man who supports his old mother. Heaven will not allow me to live if I do this. No! No! I will forgive this man." He took his foot off Li, the Devil, who saluted him. "I will let you off," said Li K'wei, "but in future you must not make use of my name."

"As you have spared my life," said Li the Devil, "I will give up this kind of life and earn an honest living in some other way."

"You are a filial son," said Li K'wei, "so I will give you ten ounces of silver to enable you to start a business." He did this, and then went on his way.

Li K'wei could not help laughing. "That fellow was quite in my hands, and yet I have started him on a fresh life." He walked on, and about 10 a.m. he was both thirsty and hungry. The footpath was quite isolated without a single house within sight. But after going some distance he saw two small straw huts a long way off. He went towards the huts, and when near he saw a woman come from behind the hut. She had a flower in her hair, and was well rouged. He spoke to her, "Sister, I am a traveler, and cannot come across an inn. I am very hungry. If you can supply me with food and wine I will pay you well."

The woman dared not refuse this when she saw the build of Li K'wei. "I have no wine, but can find you a little food."

"That will do," said Li K'wei. "Let me have a good meal as I am very hungry."

"Will a peck of rice be enough?" she asked.

"Three pecks would be better."

The woman took the rice, washed it in the stream, and then boiled it. While she was doing this Li K'wei went to the back of the house to relieve his bowels and there saw a man trudging along. Just then the woman came out of the back door to get some vegetables, and she asked the man, "What is the trouble with your leg?"

"I very nearly cannot see you again," replied the man. "I was very unlucky. I went to that place, and waited nearly a fortnight for a traveler to pass, but there was nothing doing. To-day, however, a traveler arrived, but do you think who it was? It was Li K'wei, the Black Whirlwind! It was a strange occurrence that I should meet him on such a quiet byroad. He knocked me down with a blow of his sword, and intended to kill me. But I deceived him by saying, 'If you kill me, you will kill two.' He asked me for an explanation, and I told him falsely that I had an old mother at home who depended on my support. If I was killed she would die of hunger. The fool believed me, and spared my life. He even gave me money to turn over a new leaf. So when he let me go I did not come straight here as he might have found me out, but instead I went up the hills and made a long detour."

"Don't talk so loudly!" the woman said. "A man came here, and asked for some food and it may be the same man. He is sitting outside the front door. You go and have a look at him. If he is the same man then go and get some drug to put in his food, and when it takes effect we can kill him. We can then get his money, which will enable us to live in the town and enter into trade—much better than being mere highwayman here."

Li K'wei thought, "What a rascal! I spared his life, and even gave him money, and yet he plans to kill me. Heaven cannot allow such man to live!" He went round the corner to the back door where they were talking. As soon as Li the Devil saw Li K'wei he tried to escape, but Li K'wei seized hold of him. The woman saw this, and went through the house to the front door. Li K'wei knocked Li the Devil on the ground, and then taking his sword cut off the man's head. He then went inside the house to seize the woman, but she had disappeared. He however searched in the rooms, found the place where they kept the money and woman's ornaments, and he took these. He noticed that the rice was well boiled, but there were no vegetables. When he had eaten enough, he placed the corpse in the house and set the whole place on fire. He then continued on his way, and reached his village of Tung Tien Tung about 5 p.m. He soon found his home, pushed open the door and entered. His mother called out from her bed, "Who is that?" Li K'wei saw that his mother was blind, and was sitting on the bed reciting her prayers. He called out, "Mother! Your Iron Ox has returned!"

"My boy, you have been absent for a long time. Where have you been employed? Your elder brother works as a servant, but the wages he gets are hardly enough to support us. I have often thought of you, and have weeped so much that I have become blind in both eyes. What are you doing now?"

Li K'wei thought, "If I tell her that I am a brigand from Liang Shan Po she will not go with me. I must tell her some fibs." So he said, "Mother, I am in government employment, and have come to take you away with me."

"Splendid! But how can I go?"

"I will carry you on my back to the road where we can find a cart."

"Well, wait until your elder brother comes, and then we will discuss the matter."

"Why wait?" asked Li K'wei. "I am going with you."

Just then it happened that his elder brother Li Ta entered the room carrying an earthenware jar containing rice for his mother. When Li K'wei saw his brother he kotowed and said, "Brother, I have not seen you for years."

Li Ta spoke abusively, "Why have you returned? Much trouble you will bring here again?"

His mother answered, "Your brother is now in government employment, and has specially come to take me away with him."

"Mother! Don't believe his nonsense," said Li Ta. "Some time ago he killed a man, and I was arrested, and wore a cangue for it. I have had much suffering for him. I have heard that he has joined the brigands at Liang Shan Po, and recently rescued some of them from an execution ground at Chiang Chou. A warrant is out for his arrest, and as they have not found him they wanted to arrest me. My master pleaded for me at the yamen, and said that my brother Li K'wei left home ten years ago, and we have not heard anything of him since then. He thought that perhaps the bandits were using the name of Li K'wei falsely. My master gave money to the officials at the yamen, and that is why they have not arrested me. A proclamation has been issued offering a reward of three thousand strings of cash for the arrest of my brother, Li K'wei. Now, he returns home, and talks nonsense to you."

"Do not worry," replied Li K'wei. "How would it be if we all went to Liang Shan Po, and had a good time there?"

Li Ta was angry at this, and tried to strike his brother, but was aware that he could not overcome him. He then threw the earthenware jar on the floor, and ran out of the room.

"He has gone to report my arrival," said Li K'wei to himself, "so I must leave at once before they arrive to arrest me. My brother has never seen much money so I will leave fifty ounces of silver on the bed for him. When he sees it he will not be so keen to witness my arrest." He did this and said, "Mother! I will now carry you on my back."

"Where are you going to?" she asked.

"You need not ask, anyhow it is a much better place than this," said Li K'wei. He then lifted his mother on his back, and left the house with her.

Now Li Ta had run and informed his master of the return of his brother, and soon came back with about ten farm laborers. When he entered the room he found nothing but a piece of silver on the bed. He then considered, "My brother has left this money for me. Where can he hide now? He may come with other men from Liang Shan Po. If I try to overtake him I shall only get into trouble."

As the laborers could not find Li K'wei they did not know what to do, but Li Ta told them, "My brother has evidently gone, and carried off my mother. There are many byroads about here, but how can we find which way he has gone." The men saw that Li Ta did not know what to do so after a rest they all returned to the farm.

Li K'wei, carrying his mother on his back, chose the quietest paths, and towards evening arrived at the foot of a range of mountains. He recognized the place as I Ling, and knew that if he crossed the range there were farmhouses on the other side. The moonlight was bright, and he had no difficulty in slowly ascending the mountain path. His mother asked him to find some water as she was quite thirsty, and Li K'wei assured her that as soon as they had crossed the mountain he would find a house where they could rest and get food. His mother replied that at the last meal she had had only dry rice without any liquid, and so was very thirsty. He replied, "My throat also burns like a fire, and my breath is like smoke issuing from my mouth. You wait until I get to the summit when I will have a look around for some water."

"I feel as though I must die. I am so thirsty," said his mother.

"I am getting very tired, mother," replied Li K'wei.

When he reached the summit he put his mother down by the side of a big green bowlder, and left his sword there, and went off to look for water. He soon heard the sound of running water, and after a few turns he came to a small stream. He had a good drink, using his hands as a cup, and then thought, "How can I carry some water to my mother?" He looked around on all sides, and at last espied a temple in the distance. He made his way there through the dense bushes. At last he reached the temple, and saw that it was called, "The Ta Shen Temple of Ssu Chou." In front of it was a stone incense urn, and he seized hold of it with the idea of using it to carry the water. But the stone urn was one solid piece with the base, and he could not move it. At this he got angry and using his full strength at last rooted the stone out of the ground. He then lifted it, and broke the top part from the base on the stone steps leading up to it.

He carried the stone urn off to the stream where he thoroughly washed it, and cleaned it out with grass. He then half filled it with water, and carried it off in both hands. He followed the same way back, but had great difficulties in making his way with such an awkward load. When he reached the big green bowlder, however, he was astounded not to see his mother although his sword was still there. He called out aloud for her, but there was no response. He became very anxious, as although he looked all around carefully he could find no traces or clue of her departure. But when he had gone a distance of about thirty steps he found the grass covered with blood. He trembled with fear now, but followed the marks. These at last brought him to a cave where he saw two tiger cubs inside eating a human leg. Shaking with anger he thought, "I came from Liang Shan Po to take my mother, and carried her here on my back, but it seems that she has been eaten by the tigers." His mind was inflamed with passion, and his face glared with a fierce look—his moustaches standing out like porcupine's quills. Seizing his sword he slashed at the tiger cubs. They growled, showed their teeth and claws as they reared on their hind legs, and rushed at him. He killed one with a single cut of his sword, and the other cub retreated to the cave. Li K'wei followed with sword in hand and killed the second cub. He then turned round and saw the tigress outside racing towards the cave. He said, "So you are the beast who has devoured my mother." He threw down his long sword, and took the dagger from his waist. The tigress stopped at the entrance, lashing its tail from side to side, and not having seen Li K'wei, turned round facing outside. Li K'wei jumped forward, and stabbed the beast in the hind-quarters—a mighty lunge typical of the rage that he felt. The tigress roared, and leapt away with the dagger sticking in her body, and galloped away. Li K'wei picked up his sword and left the cave. As the tigress had galloped off wounded a strong wind sprung up, shook the trees as in a big storm. There is an ancient saying, "Clouds originate with dragons, whereas winds originate with tigers." At that spot the moonlight was quite bright, and suddenly there was a tremendous roar, and a tiger leapt forth. It rushed at Li K'wei, who deliberately and without fear, slashed with his sword, and cut its throat as it sprang at him. The tiger feeling the pain, and finding breathing difficult, retreated a few steps, and then as it expired gave forth its last roar which sounded something like a landslide of half a mountain. Li K'wei had now killed four tigers, and he now entered the tigers' den in the cave, looking carefully to see whether there was still another one. Having found nothing there and being tired, he made his way back to the temple, and slept there that night. The next day he collected the remains and torn clothing of his mother, and buried them behind the temple. He could not avoid crying while doing this. He felt very hungry now, and continued his way across the range of mountains. He soon met five hunters armed with crossbows and arrows. Li K'wei's clothes were all covered with blood, and this sight startled the hunters. They asked, "Are you a guardian spirit of this mountain? How otherwise dare you cross the range?"

Li K'wei thought, "I cannot tell them who I am because there is a reward offered for my arrest." So he replied, "I am a traveler, and last night I was crossing the mountain with my mother. While I went to get some water for her a tiger attacked and ate her. So I found the tiger's den, and there killed two cubs, and afterwards two fully grown tigers. I slept last night in the Ta Shen Temple and have just come from there."

"We don't believe that," cried the hunters. "How could one man kill four tigers? We might believe you killing two cubs, but to kill two fully grown tigers is really a big achievement. We have been beaten by the officials for not killing those two tigers. Those tigers have been on the mountains for a long time, and during the last five months nobody has dared go that way. We do not believe what you say! You need not try to humbug us."

"I do not belong to this district," said Li K'wei. "Why should I humbug you? If you don't believe me then I will go and show you the dead tigers, and you can get them carried down the mountain."

"If this is true we shall be much indebted to you," said the hunters. They blew whistles, and soon about fifty men had assembled at that spot. They got poles and ropes, and then all accompanied Li K'wei up the mountain. There sure enough they found the bodies of the four tigers, and carried them down the mountain. The hunters reported the matter to the head of the first village they came to, and they then all adjourned to the big house of the local wealthy man—Mr. Ts'ao. This man was a clerk in the district yamen, and had made his wealth by extortion in his own village. He was disliked and also feared by his own neighbors. Yet he was always talking of loyalty and filial piety so that he was well known as a hypocrite. As soon as he heard what had happened he invited Li K'wei into the hall where he asked for full details of the remarkable event. Aftert his had all been recited he asked for the name and home address of Li K'wei.

"My name is Chang," replied Li K'wei, "but people generally call me 'Courageous Chang.' "

"You are certainly courageous," said Mr. Ts'ao, "if you had not a large gall you could not have killed four tigers." He then gave orders for a big feast to be provided in honor to the "Courageous Chang."

It was soon known in the villages around that four tigers had been killed by one man and in no time the people were crowding into the village, and into Mr. Ts'ao's house to see the tigers There they gazed at the great hero who was being entertained in the hall by Mr. Ts'ao. Among the people was the wife of Li the Devil, whose husband Li K'wei had killed a few days ago. She had run away to her parents' home and when she heard the news about the tigers she followed the crowd. She recognized Li K'wei and immediately returned home and reported the matter to her parents. They went at once to the local Ti Pao who was given to know that Li K'wei was the criminal for whose arrest a reward had been offered. He secretly sent a messenger asking Mr. Ts'ao to come and discuss a very urgent matter. When Mr. Ts'ao received the message he decided not to tell Li K'wei, but merely said that he wished to retire and change his clothes, but when outside the room he hurried straight off to the other village.

"This man who has killed the tigers," said the Ti Pao, "is Li K'wei, the Black Whirlwind of Po Chang Village, and there is a summon out for his arrest."

"In that case you must make careful inquiries among the people, and make sure of the matter before we act. It will be an easy matter to arrest him when we are sure about his identity. If he is not the man then we should only make trouble by arresting him."

"There is a woman here, Mrs. Li, who recognizes him," said Ti Pao. "He came to her house and later he killed her husband."

"As that appears to be conclusive," said Mr. Ts'ao, "we had better entertain him at the feast, and then ask him whether he prefers to go to the magistrate and ask for a reward for killing the tigers, or whether he prefers to receive the reward in our village. If he objects to go to the magistrate for the reward we can assume that he is guilty. Then we must press him to take plenty of wine and get him drunk when we can easily tie him up. Then we can go to the magistrate yamen and ask them to send a police inspector to arrest him and so there can be no failure."

The Ti Pao agreed to this and made arrangements accordingly with his men. Mr. Ts'ao returned home and there resumed his seat at the table with Li K'wei. He said, "I hope you are not offended at my leaving you. Please make yourself quite at home. Loosen your dress and put your dagger at one side."

"I left my dagger in the belly of one of the tigers," said Li K'wei, "and only have the scabbard here. When they cut the tiger open I hope they will find my dagger and return it to me."

"Never mind that!" said Mr. Ts'ao. "I have a very good sword here which I will present to you."

Li K'wei thereupon took off the scabbard, and belt and handed them to a servant. Mr. Ts'ao ordered a fresh supply of food and wine. The Ti Pao, the hunters and several other men were present at the feast, and they each in turn toasted Li K'wei. During the feast Mr. Ts'ao asked Li K'wei whether he would prefer to receive the reward for killing the tigers at the magistrate yamen or in that village.

"I am only a traveler," said Li K'wei, "and have hardly time to go to the magistrate. I just happened to kill the tigers on my way, and do not care to go to the magistrate. I will receive the reward here, but even if there is no reward I can leave without it."

"We do not care to treat you disrespectfully," said Mr. Ts'ao, "so you must at least wait until we have collected the money to present you. We will send the tigers to the magistrate yamen."

"Could you first give me a change of clothing," asked Li K'wei, "as these clothes are rather soiled."

Mr. Ts'ao agreed to this and ordered a servant to bring a suit of blue cloth. Li K'wei took the new clothes, and when he had changed he was met outside the door of the hall by many men who also wished to drink a cup of wine with him. One cup of wine was warm, another was cold, and so on. Li K'wei did not suspect any plot, and drank freely with great joviality. He had now quite forgotten Sung Chiang's order that he was not to drink wine. It was not very long before he was dead drunk. The men then removed him to a small empty room at the back where they stretched him on a bench, and then bound him to the bench with ropes. The Ti Pao then sent urgent messengers to report the matter to the magistrate yamen. He also had an accusation drawn up for Mrs. Li who accompanied the messenger to the yamen.

When the magistrate heard the report he was startled and asked, "Where has the Black Whirlwind been arrested? We must not allow this rebel to escape!"

The messenger and the hunters told him that Li K'wei was imprisoned in Mr. Ts'ao's house in their village. They were afraid that he might escape, and did not dare to try to bring him to the yamen. The magistrate summoned inspector Li Yun to the court, and instructed him to take a large body of policemen to Mr. Ts'ao's house and arrest the prisoner Li K'wei, the Black Whirlwind. He was to exercise great care, and be sure that the prisoner did not escape.

Inspector Li Yun got together about thirty of his most trusted men, armed them and departed for the village. The Hsien was only a small place so that everybody knew what was happening. Now the news soon reached the village on the east side of the town where Chu Kwei was living with his brother. Chu Kwei spoke to his brother, "That fellow Li K'wei is evidently in trouble. What shall we do to save him? I was specially deputed by Sung Chiang to come here, and watch the proceedings, Li K'wei will be arrested, but if I do not save his life how can I go back and face our elder brother Sung Chiang? What shall we do?"

"Do not get excited," said Chu Fu. "This inspector Li Yun is a skilled military man, and fifty men cannot rival him. You and I are no match against him although we worked together on the same plan. We must use strategy and not force. Now inspector Li Yun is a close personal friend of mine, and every day he has been training me in the use of military weapons. I have a plan, but it will prevent our living in this place any more. We must boil about twenty pounds of meat and cut it up into large pieces and prepare about ten jars of wine. In both of these we must mix some sleeping drug. About 4 a.m. we must start off with our assistants carrying the food and wine and wait in a quiet spot on the road for Li Yun. When he arrives we must offer him and his men the food and wine as a gift, and get them all senseless. Then we can release Li K'wei and escape."

"That is a splendid plan," said Chu Kwei, "and we will get things ready at once."

"Inspector Li Yun does not drink wine," said Chu Fu, "and as he will only take the drugged meat he will probably recover consciousness before the others. As soon as he finds out how we have deceived him it will not be safe for any of us to stay here."

"You are an innkeeper here," said Chu Kwei, "but you do not make much money. It would be better if you can go with me to Liang Shan Po and join the brigands there, and get much money and new clothing and enjoy life generally, We can tell two of your servants to get a cart, load up your valuables with your wife, and send them on in advance to wait for us at a village called Shih Li Pai."

"Brother, that is a good idea," replied Chu Fu. He arranged matters accordingly, and it was not long before the cart had started on its way.

That evening the two brothers boiled the meat and mixed the drug in same. They also prepared the wine in the same way. The whole supply was made up into two loads, and they also took about thirty cups with them. The two servants and the two brothers divided the loads. They got away about 4 a.m. and halted when they came to a quiet desolate spot on the road. It was just dawn when they heard the sound of gongs approaching, and Chu Kwei went forward by himself to meet the party. It was inspector Li Yun with his men escorting the prisoner Li K'wei, the Black Whirlwind, to the town. Inspector Li Yun was riding a horse in the rear of his party. As they came up to Chu Fu he called out, "Sir, I request you to stop, and accept a little refreshment." He at once offered Li Yun wine while Chu Kwei passed round the meat. Upon seeing this inspector Li Yun quickly dismounted and hurrying to the front spoke to Chu Fu, "Friend, why have you come so far as this to entertain us?"

"I wish to give you a little comfort," replied Chu Fu. He saw that inspector Li Yun was not drinking the wine so he continued, "I am aware that you are a teetotaler but I particularly request you to take a little liquor this time."

Inspector Li Yun did not like to refuse this pressing offer so he took a few sips. Chu Fu then pressed him to take a little meat, but inspector Li Yun declined this as he said he had had a big dinner last night.

"But you have a long way to go," replied Chu Fu, "and you will be hungry before you reach your destination. Please take a little at least and so save my face with your men."

Here again inspector Li Yun did not like to cause annoyance by declining the offer, so he ate some of the meat. All the policemen also partook of the wine and the meat, and Chu Kwei even offered it to all the villagers who were following the party. Without making inquiries as to whether it was hot or cold they all set to and had a good feed. They all took it in a happy-go-lucky style and no questions were raised.

Li K'wei seeing Chu Kwei and his brother knew that this was some trick so he said, "Are you not going to give me some of this stuff?"

"Why should we? You are only a mere criminal," replied Chu Kwei. "You had better shut your mouth as you have not long to live."

Just then inspector Li Yun saw that his men were looking at each other stupidly and could not move so he exclaimed, "We have been fooled by a ruse." He tried to move, but instead he also fell down and was soon asleep.

Chu Kwei and Chu Fu seizing their swords now shouted out, "Let no man depart!" Some men however tried to get away, but they were soon caught and killed on the spot. Li K'wei seeing this burst asunder the ropes and taking a sword went up to inspector Li Yun to kill him. But Chu Fu stopped him, "Do not kill him! He is my teacher, and is an extremely good man."

"Then let me at least kill that ass, Mr. Ts'ao," said Li K'wei. He went forward and found Mr. Ts'ao and the wife of Li the Devil, he killed both of them. He also killed the hunters, the Ti Pao, and all the soldiers. He then stripped a soldier of his uniform and put it on himself. The three men then left the scene by a small side path. But Chu Fu soon stopped and said, "How can I leave like this? Inspector Li Yun was my teacher, but how can he face the magistrate alone when all his men have been slaughtered? He must come to pursue us when he recovers consciousness, and I will wait for him and suggest to him to escape with me and join the bandits at Liang Shan Po."

Chu Kwei said, "Younger brother, what you say is quite

true. I will go forward and join the cart. Li K'wei will stop here with you and wait for him. But if inspector Li Yun will not come with you then you must not insist on waiting for him."

"I agree," said Chu Fu. Chu Kwei then departed.

Chu Fu and Li K'wei sat down and after about two hours they saw inspector Li Yun rushing towards them with a sword in his hand and shouting, "You brigands shall not escape." Li K'wei saw that inspector Li Yun was furious and fearing that he might strike Chu Fu, stood up, with his sword to fight with inspector Li Yun.

Liang Shan Po gains two tigers,
And welcomes and fêtes four men.